EV

JUDI CURTIN grew up in Cork and now lives in Limerick where she is married with three children. Judi is the author of *Eva's Journey*, as well as the best-selling 'Alice & Megan' series. With Roisin Meaney, she is the author of *See If I Care*, and she has written three novels, *Sorry, Walter*, *From Claire to Here* and *Almost Perfect*. Her books have sold into Serbian, Portuguese, German, Russian, Lithuanian and most recently to Australia and New Zealand.

The 'Alice & Megan' series
Alice Next Door
Alice Again
Don't Ask Alice
Alice in the Middle
Bonjour Alice
Alice & Megan Forever
Alice to the Rescue
Alice & Megan's Cookbook

Other books
Eva's Journey
See If I Care (with Roisin Meaney)

Praise for the 'Alice & Megan' series
'If you like Jacqueline Wilson, then you'll love Judi Curtin!' *Primary Times*

'Judi Curtin's "Alice" books celebrate friendship, humour and loyalty.' *Sunday Independent*

Judi Curtin

EVA'S HOLIDAY

THE O'BRIEN PRESS
DUBLIN

First published 2011 by The O'Brien Press Ltd,
12 Terenure Road East, Rathgar, Dublin 6, Ireland.
Tel: +353 1 4923333; Fax: +353 1 4922777
E-mail: books@obrien.ie
Website: www.obrien.ie

ISBN: 978-1-84717-280-8

A catalogue record for this title is available from the British Library

1 2 3 4 5 6 7 8
11 12 13 14

The O'Brien Press receives assistance from

Layout and design: The O'Brien Press Ltd
Cover illustration: Woody Fox
Printed and bound by CPI Group (UK) Ltd
The paper used in this book is produced using pulp from managed forests

For Dan, Brian, Ellen and Annie

Chapter One

'This is so totally unfair. This is the worst thing that has ever happened to me.'

I punched the pillow I was holding, but it didn't make me feel any better. *Nothing* could make me feel any better.

I was in my bedroom, with my friends, Victoria, Ella and Ruby. I'd just told them about my mum and dad's great plans for the summer.

I punched the pillow again. 'Well?' I said.

'Maybe it won't be too bad,' said Victoria. 'And you might even enjoy it. You—'

'I am *so* not going to enjoy it,' I said, interrupting her. 'Remember, I'm used to spending my holidays in a villa in Tuscany. How am I supposed to enjoy a trip to a stupid old cottage, in a stupid old village in the middle of nowhere? What am I supposed to *do* all day long? I won't have any friends. There won't be any shops or a cinema. There's nothing there – a big fat nothing! I might as well just sit inside and wait for summer to be over.'

Victoria ignored me. 'Maybe I can come and visit you for a while.'

'Yeah right. If you can fit it in between all your fun pony camps and holidays to cool places that a normal human being would actually want to visit.'

'Maybe Ella—' she began.

Ella shook her head.

'Sorry, Eva. I'd love to visit you, but I'll be spending most of the summer helping my dad run his summer camp. Maybe Ruby?'

I knew exactly what Ella was thinking. Ruby doesn't really like the same kind of stuff as

Victoria, Ella and I do. She wasn't likely to have big plans for the summer.

We all looked at her.

Ruby went red.

'Actually, I haven't got much free time this summer,' she said. 'I did kind of well in my last gala, so I've got scholarships to a few swimming camps.'

'That's brilliant!' Victoria and I said together as Ella leaned over to hug her.

Ruby wriggled free, embarrassed – she totally hates being the centre of attention.

'Let's get back to talking about Eva's summer,' she said.

'Don't bother,' I said. 'It's too boring. This summer, I'm going to be the biggest loser in the whole country.'

Victoria patted my arm like I was a baby. 'I'll lend you my blue hoodie that you like so much, and I bet if you're really lucky, Ella will lend you one of her totally cool summer tops.'

Ella nodded from where she was perched at the end of my bed.

'Sure I will, Eva,' she said. 'You can borrow anything you want.'

'And I'll ask my mum to make you a special bracelet,' said Ruby.

Ella sighed.

'I think I'd endure a summer in the country for one of your mum's amazing bracelets, Ruby,' she said.

'Want to swap?' I said.

Ella shook her head quickly, 'Er … maybe not.'

'Anyway, thanks for your kind offers,' I said. 'But you'll all be wasting your time. What's the point in wearing cool stuff when there's no one cool around to see you?'

Once again, Victoria ignored me.

'The summer isn't all that long, really,' she said

I was fed up of punching the pillow. Now I felt like punching my so-called friend.

Couldn't she see that a summer in a cottage in the country was like a life sentence?

Why did she always have to see the bright side?

Didn't she understand that I wanted her to feel sorry for me?

I turned to Ella. She usually has less to say than Victoria has, but mostly she makes a lot of sense.

'What do you think, Ella?' I asked.

Ella thought for a while before speaking.

'Well,' she said slowly. 'There is one *really* good thing.'

'What's that?' I asked.

'I'm just glad it's not me.'

✵ ♥ ♡

The next day, Ruby had a swimming gala, and Ella and I went to Victoria's place.

'Things have got even worse again,' I said, as soon as we were settled on the huge, squashy couch in Victoria's bedroom.

'Is that possible?' asked Victoria.

I nodded grimly. 'You see, the whole holiday thing came about because Dad did an attic conversion for Mum's friend Monica. Monica was so pleased with his work that she said we can go and stay in the cottage she bought a few months ago. We don't have to pay or anything. Dad just has to do any odd jobs that need doing while we're there.'

'That was nice of Monica,' said Victoria.

'Was it?' I said.

'And the bad news is?' prompted Ella.

'Monica has to go to hospital soon for a hip operation.'

'Ouch,' said Ella. 'I can see why that makes things bad for her, but how does it change things for you?'

'Monica has an eight-year-old son, and there won't be anyone to mind him during the day, while his dad's at work, so he's coming to the cottage with us. We get the house and we get the son – it's turned into a package deal!'

'Maybe it won't be so bad,' said Victoria. 'You're always saying that you'd like a little brother or sister.'

'I know,' I said. 'But that was before I met Joey. He's a total pain. A summer with him will be a complete nightmare.'

'And how come your mum didn't tell you this yesterday?'

Ella giggled. 'Maybe she thought you couldn't cope with all that good news at once,' she said.

I sighed. 'Who cares anyway? Joey's coming with us, and nothing I say or do is going to change that. Summer is now officially spoiled.'

Chapter Two

A few weeks later, we were packed up in Dad's van and on our way – Mum, Dad, Joey and me. Even though Victoria and Ella had been really nice, and had lent me lots of their cool clothes, and Ruby's mum had made me the most amazing bracelet, I still felt like this was the worst thing that had ever happened to me.

Mum was happy because she was getting her own way (as usual).

Joey was happy because he's only a stupid eight-year-old and it's easy to make him happy.

And Dad was happy because he knew that if he got a call to do an attic conversion, he'd be able to escape back to the real world.

As we drove along, Mum kept going on and on about how excited she was.

'We're so lucky to be able to stay in Monica's house,' she said. 'If it weren't for Monica, we'd have no holiday at all this year. We'd be stuck at home for the whole summer.'

Right then, being stuck at home sounded like a *great* option.

Suddenly I had a brilliant idea.

'Dad, if you get a call to go back to work, can I come with you?'

'No way!' said Mum.

Why did she have to get involved? I hadn't been asking her.

'Please, Dad? I'd be really good while you are at work. I could clean the house every day, and I'd make you lovely breakfasts and dinners and everything.'

I was sure I'd be the perfect housewife.

Joey interrupted, 'My mum told me that you cooked dinner last week and your whole family had to go to Supermac's afterwards because no one could eat the stuff you made.'

Why couldn't he just mind his own business? I leaned over and made a face at him. He wailed like a total baby, '*Paulaaaa*, Eva's threatening me!'

Mum turned around and waved her finger at me.

'Now, Eva,' she said. 'That's exactly why you couldn't go back home with Dad. You're not mature enough yet.'

Then she sighed.

'Come on, Eva,' she said. 'Help us out here. You know we've all had a difficult time recently, with Dad's old business closing down, and us having to sell our lovely house. And you were so good and helpful when all of that happened. Why are you being so difficult now?'

'Did you ever hear of the last straw?' I muttered. 'Well, this is it. This is the last straw.'

'Lucky you're not a camel, so,' said Dad,

thinking he was very funny.

Everyone laughed then, except for me. I just folded my arms and sat in silence while Dad kept on driving towards the end of the world.

✮　♥　♡

After another half an hour I was *totally* fed up. Joey had fallen asleep with his head on my shoulder, and every time I tried to move him away, he wailed loudly, making Mum cross with me all over again.

Suddenly I had an idea. I took Joey's notebook and pencil out of his rucksack. I found a blank page, and wrote in capital letters – 'PLEASE HELP ME. I AM BEING KIDNAPPED.' Then I held the page against the side window of the van so that everyone who passed by could see what total losers my parents were.

I thought it was kind of a funny thing to do, but I didn't feel one bit like laughing when a police motor-bike with flashing lights came past and made Dad pull in to the edge of the road.

The policeman got off his bike and walked very slowly towards us. I shoved Joey's notebook under my seat. Joey woke up.

'Wow………Coooool,' he said when he saw the flashing lights.

'Have you been speeding again?' Mum asked Dad.

Before Dad could answer, the policeman was tapping on the side window of the van. Dad wound down the window.

'What can I do for you, officer?' he said, like someone from a very bad film.

The policeman didn't smile.

'We've had a very strange report from a woman in the town a few miles back,' he said.

I tried to shrink back into my seat, wondering if there was any way of making myself invisible.

The policeman leaned closer to Dad. 'Can you tell me who you are, and please also identify your passengers.'

I felt like screaming.

What kind of a stupid woman with no sense of humour would think I was really being kidnapped?

And what kind of a policeman with no sense of humour would have to get sent to investigate?

And what kind of parents would have so little sense of humour that they would *totally* fail to see the funny side of what I'd done?

It took twenty minutes of explanations before we were allowed to continue on our journey. By then, Mum had my phone in her handbag, and I had a feeling I wouldn't be seeing it again for a very long time.

If there was a funny side to that, then I'm afraid I was the one who couldn't see it.

Chapter Three

After another half hour of driving, Joey was sound asleep again. Dad drove down a narrow laneway and stopped the van. Mum, Dad and I climbed out and stretched. We gazed at the cottage, and then we gazed at it some more. No one said anything for a long time.

The cottage was a complete and utter dump. The walls were all grey and mouldy-looking, the windows looked like the next gust of wind would blow them out, and the garden was like something from a horror movie.

'You're sure this is the right place?' said Dad after a while.

'We followed Monica's directions to the letter,'

said Mum. 'But…….'

'This has to be the wrong….' I began, but I stopped as Joey suddenly hurtled from the car and started to jump up and down on the lumpy lawn.

'Yay! We're here at last,' he shouted, crushing the last of my hopes.

'Lovely,' said Dad weakly. 'The cottage of lost dreams.'

Mum gave him a cross look, but she couldn't really argue with him. She pulled a key from her pocket and unlocked the door.

The four of us stepped inside. I shut my eyes and counted to ten. Unfortunately, when I opened my eyes, nothing had changed. We were in a room full of junk. A crooked table was surrounded by five wobbly chairs of varying sizes and colours. A dusty-looking dresser was covered with odd cups and saucers. An old sofa looked like it was about to burst open, spraying the room with grey foam. Over by the only window were a rusty sink and a tiny cooker about the size of the one I used to play with when I was five.

Joey ran across the room and threw himself onto an ugly armchair that looked like it might once have been green.

'Home sweet home,' he said, before he began to choke on the cloud of dust he'd raised.

I'd have laughed, if I hadn't been so close to crying.

'I wonder what the other rooms are like,' said Mum brightly.

I looked through an open door into a room that contained nothing but a huge lumpy bed and lots of cobwebs. I ran upstairs and discovered two more bedrooms and a bathroom. I ran downstairs again. There were so many things I wanted to say, I didn't know where to start.

Dad was poking the window and watching how it rattled at every touch.

'You can't act all surprised, Andrew,' said

Mum. 'Monica did warn us that the cottage needed fixing up a bit.'

'The kindest thing would be to knock the whole place down, and put it out of its misery,' said Dad, laughing.

He stopped laughing though, when he saw Mum's face.

'Oh,' he said. 'I'll get my toolbox out of the van and I can start work at once.'

I started to smile. Dad absolutely loves fixing stuff.

But then I had a horrible thought. I gazed frantically around the room.

'Where's the TV?'

'Oh,' said Mum. 'Didn't I tell you?'

'Tell me *what*?' I said in my toughest voice.

'About the TV.'

'What about the TV?'

Mum gave a little laugh, 'There isn't one.'

Was this Mum's idea of a joke? Did she really think we were going to stay here for a whole summer, without even a TV to console us?

She came over and hugged me.

'Don't worry, Eva,' she said. 'All this place needs is a good clean out, and then it will be lovely. And we'll all have the time of our lives.'

✳   ♥   ♡

We unpacked the car, and after that, Mum and Dad insisted that we all go for a walk on the beach. The beach was small and not very exciting, and I was almost glad when Mum said it was time to get back to work.

We spent the rest of the day scrubbing and cleaning. Finally when there was nothing left to clean, Mum and Dad let us sit down. I looked around the small room.

'That's a big improvement,' I said. 'Before, it was dirty and ugly, and now it's clean and ugly.'

Mum looked pointedly at Joey.

'Shh, Eva,' she said. 'Don't say things like

that, since Monica was so kind to let us use her house.'

'I won't "shhh",' I said, not caring what Joey thought. 'You always say I have to tell the truth, and the truth is this place is a total dump.'

Joey opened his eyes wide, but for once in his life, he said nothing.

Dad tried to comfort me.

'It's not so bad, Eva,' he said. 'Money is still very tight, and what your mother said earlier is true – if we weren't here, we'd have no holiday at all this year.'

'No holiday at all would be better than a holiday from hell,' I shouted.

'Eva!' said Mum crossly. 'If you can't think of something nice to say, it's better to say nothing at all.'

Dad laughed. 'Looks like it's going to be a quiet summer so,' he said.

I said a rude word then, and was sent to bed.

And that was the first day of my holidays.

Chapter Four

The next morning, I woke to the sound of hammering. By the time I was dressed, Dad had fixed the crooked table and the wobbly chairs, and was pacing the living room with a screwdriver in his hand.

'That's enough for the moment, Andrew,' said Mum, laughing. 'Come and join us for breakfast.'

'So,' said Dad as he sat down. 'What's the plan for today?'

'I *had* thought we could have a picnic on the beach,' said Mum. 'But I think maybe it's a bit grey and cold for that.'

'Well,' I said. 'Since we can't go to the beach,

let's think of something else to do. We could look out the front window, or we could look out the back window or we could walk to the stupid village, or we could … oh yeah that's it, isn't it? That's everything we can do in this stupid place.'

Mum put on her dangerous face.

'Now, Eva,…' she began, before she was interrupted by a knock on the front door.

We all looked at each other.

'Are we expecting someone?' asked Dad.

'Not that I know of,' said Mum.

'Maybe it's my fairy godmother, come to rescue me,' I said. 'I wonder where I left my pumpkin?'

No one laughed.

'Do you know any of the neighbours here, Joey?' asked Mum.

Joey shook his head.

'I've only been here once before,' he said.

There was another knock.

Joey stood up.

'*I'll* go,' he said in a bored voice, like he'd done nothing except answer the door all morning.

He opened the door and stood there for a second. Then he closed the door and ran back over to us.

'There's someone out there, but I don't know if it's a boy or a girl,' he whispered.

'What did they want?' asked Dad.

Joey shrugged, 'Dunno. Didn't ask did I? I was too busy trying to decide what it was.'

Mum nudged me.

'Go and see who it is, there's a love.'

I sighed and got up and went to the door. Our visitor was still standing on the step. She was a girl, but I could see why Joey had been confused. She had short, untidy hair that looked like it had been cut by a blind hairdresser. She was dressed in what looked like a boy's tracksuit, and runners. She looked about my age. She stared at me, and I stared back at her.

'Hello,' I said, as 'hi' seemed a bit too friendly for this strange, silent person.

'Hello,' she said back, and then we looked at each other some more.

I was starting to feel a bit embarrassed.

Would it be rude to say, *what do you want?*

In the end I couldn't take any more. 'Can I help you?' I asked, sounding like somebody's ancient old granny.

The girl looked like she was about to laugh.

Was she going to laugh at *me*?

I was wearing Victoria's blue hoodie, and one of Ella's totally cool tops, so how dare someone wearing a boy's tracksuit laugh at me?

'I don't need help, thanks,' she said.

And there was another long silence.

This was totally stupid.

'I'll go inside, so,' I said.

Now the girl went red.

'No! Don't go. I live over there,' she said, pointing vaguely in the direction of our hedge.

'I saw you arriving yesterday.'

Oh no!

Had she heard me shouting at Mum and Dad and acting like a total baby?

I could feel my face going red now, giving me something in common with this strange girl.

Then I tossed my head. Why did I care what she thought of me anyway?

'And?' I said coolly.

'… and I was wondering if you'd like to … I don't know … go for a walk or something?'

Great.

There was a crazy girl living at the other side of our hedge, and she wanted to be my friend and do totally fun stuff like going for walks.

Summer was looking up.

Not.

'I don't know,' I said. 'We've just got here, and I probably have to help my mum and dad around the house for a while. I—'

Suddenly Dad was at my shoulder.

'Who's this, Eva?' he said, like I was supposed to know.

'I'm Kate,' said the girl.

I turned and made a face at Dad. 'Kate asked me to go for a walk with her, but I was just telling her how you and Mum need me to stay here and do a few jobs for you.'

Dad beamed at me. 'Oh, that's very kind of you, Eva, but I think we'll manage without you for a while. You go off and have fun with your new friend.'

'But I haven't even had my breakfast yet!' I wailed.

Dad shoved the piece of toast he had in his hand towards me.

'Here,' he said. 'Have mine.'

I took the toast and made another face at Dad, but he ignored it. He practically pushed me outside.

'See you later,' he said, as he closed the door behind me. 'And don't rush back, we'll be absolutely fine.'

I stood outside the closed door. Part of me wanted to run around to the back of the cottage, and climb in through a window. If I did that though, I knew Mum and Dad would just make me go back out again, so I'd still have to go on the stupid walk, and I'd be in heaps of trouble as well.

I looked at Kate.

'OK' I said in my most bored voice. 'It's too cold for the beach, so where are we going to go?'

She shrugged. 'Where do you want to go?'

'Home,' I said.

I thought that was quite funny, but Kate didn't even smile.

'Let's just walk in to town, so,' she said.

There's a town?

I really wanted to know more about this town, but that would have involved having a conversation with Kate, so I bottled up my curiosity and looked bored again

Kate started walking and I walked beside her.
What else could I do?

Chapter Five

We walked along the rough, narrow road. The only sound came from the rattling of the small stone that Kate was kicking along in front of her. It was weird walking along beside this silent person. I started to feel nervous, which I knew was stupid. I was totally fed up. This was supposed to be a holiday, not an ordeal.

Talking would probably have helped, but there was no way I was starting a conversation. Kate was the one who had called for me, and had come up with the idea of this stupid walk. If she wanted to be my friend, *she* could do the talking bit.

But after what felt like half an hour, the

silence was getting to me, and I knew I couldn't take it any more.

'Have you got any brothers or sisters?' I asked.

'No.'

'Oh, me neither.'

Was I owning up to having something in common with her?

Kate didn't seem to care much, but I tried again anyway.

'Have you lived here all your life?' I asked.

'Yes,' said Kate.

'And is your school near here?'

'Yes,' she said again, not making any effort to help the conversation along.

I felt like shaking her, but even if I'd been brave enough to do it, I had a horrible feeling that she wouldn't react.

Then, without thinking, I flicked my fingers under the collar of Ella's top, and made it stand up over the neck of Victoria's hoodie. As I did this, Kate looked over at me. She reached up, and almost touched my collar, but pulled back at the last moment.

'Don't *do* that,' she said.

'Do what?' I asked.

I was confused, but glad that I'd got a reaction from her at last.

'Don't do that ... that thing with your collar.'

This was getting crazier by the second.

'Why shouldn't I?' I asked. 'Is there a law against it in this part of the world?'

Kate didn't answer for a minute, and when she did, she spoke so quietly I could hardly hear her.

'That's what *they* do.'

'Who are "they",' I asked, looking around nervously.

Kate stopped walking and glared at me.

'The cool girls. That's what they do all day long – fix their collars.'

Now I stopped walking too.

There were cool girls in this place?

Where were they?

How could I find them?

How quickly could I get away from this loser and make some proper friends?

I tried not to sound too interested.

'Er, who exactly are the "cool girls"?'

Kate gave a big long sigh.

'There are two of them. Cathy and Lily. Lily lives near here, and she goes to my school. We were best friends in Junior Infants.'

'And now?'

'Junior Infants was a long time ago,' she said.

'And Cathy?'

'Cathy comes to stay in the town for the summer. Lily's a pain all year round, but when Cathy shows up, she turns into a total nightmare.'

'What kind of a nightmare?' I asked.

If these girls were cool enough, I might be able to overlook their faults.

'They think they are *so* great,' said Kate. 'They

wear fancy clothes and they spend all day fixing their collars and admiring their nails. Years ago they used to have normal hair, but now it's shiny and they toss it around all the time.

She stopped talking and looked at me.

'At least you don't do that hair straightening thing.'

(That's because Mum had confiscated my hair-straightener the week before. Another sense of humour failure. Just because I decided to straighten the hair on that stupid porcelain doll she keeps on the mantelpiece. Just because I didn't know that instead of going all straight and shiny, the doll's hair would melt and burn and then fall out. And Mum waited until I'd spent an hour cleaning the straightener, before she took it from me.)

I suddenly remembered that my hair was all curly. I could feel my face going red again as I tried to flatten my hair with my fingers.

But then I remembered that I didn't care what

Kate thought of me, so I put my hands into my pockets.

'I take it Cathy and Lily aren't friends of yours these days?' I said.

Kate shook her head.

'No way. Who'd want to be friends with them?'

Me?

Cathy and Lily sounded like the perfect friends for me.

Kate started walking again, and I followed her.

I had made up my mind. I'd be a nice, generous girl. I'd walk wherever Kate wanted me to walk. I'd even talk to her, if that's what she wanted.

Then, as soon as I got the chance, I'd find the cool girls, make friends and that would be that.

The summer would be sorted.

Chapter Six

At last Kate stopped walking. 'This is it,' she said. 'This is town.'

'But this is the village.'

Kate didn't answer.

I looked around. We were standing on a narrow street. There were two tiny shops with buckets and shovels and beach balls hanging in the doorway, a post office, a pub with a petrol pump outside and a few brightly-painted houses.

I almost laughed. Then I saw Kate's face. She was glaring at me, almost daring me to say something bad about the place. And suddenly I felt afraid. Kate wasn't like any other girl I'd ever met. I didn't know how to act around her. I didn't know what to say. I didn't know what to do.

'What do you think?' she asked.

What did I think?

I thought that this was the most pathetic place I'd ever been to in my whole life. That's what I thought.

But what I said was, 'What do you *do* around here?'

Kate shrugged.

'Do? I don't know. What do you do where you live?'

I had to think. I'd only been gone for a day, but already, home seemed so far away, it was an effort to remember.

'Well, if I have money, I go to the cinema, or I go bowling, or I go shopping. Sometimes I just hang out with my friends.'

I felt like crying.

Ruby was already settled into her swimming

camp. I wondered what Victoria and Ella were doing now. Whatever it was, it had to be more fun than what I was doing. Everything was more fun than what I was doing.

And suddenly, I'd had enough.

'This is the biggest dump in the whole world,' I shouted. 'I'd die if I had to live here forever, and I'll probably die just from staying here for the summer.'

I knew it was rude and mean, but I couldn't stop myself. I said lots more stuff like this, only stopping when I ran out of breath.

I looked at Kate. Why wasn't she shouting back at me?

Why wasn't she defending her home?

She just folded her arms and gave me that look of hers, the one that I couldn't make any sense of.

'Let's walk back, so, will we?' she said, like I hadn't said anything bad at all.

And because I couldn't think of anything else

to do, we walked back towards our house.

'My mum's going to make me do loads of stupid jobs this afternoon,' I said after a while, trying to break the silence.

'My mum ...' began Kate, but then she stopped.

'Your mum what?' I asked.

'Nothing,' said Kate.

I didn't bother asking her again.

If she wanted to be like that, what did I care?

Kate said nothing else at all on the way back, and neither did I.

At last we were at our house. Kate and I stood outside and looked at each other. There was *no* way I was asking her in. I just wanted to be very far away from her. She was *way* too weird for me.

And suddenly I heard myself saying, 'Why don't you call over again tomorrow?'

What was all that about?

I wished I could reach out and grab the words

before they got to her ears.

Kate was *so* not the kind of girl I wanted to be friends with, so why was I asking her to call for me again?

Maybe because I felt guilty about all the bad stuff I'd said?

Kate didn't answer for ages.

'Maybe,' she said in the end. 'If I have time.'

And then she seemed to vanish into the hedge, and was gone.

Chapter Seven

After breakfast the next morning, Dad said he'd show Joey how to measure wood for new skirting boards. Joey was dancing around, all excited, like Dad had just promised to show him the secrets of the universe.

'Why don't you invite your friend over for tea tonight?' said Mum as soon as they'd gone outside.

'Because she's *so* not my friend,' I said through gritted teeth. 'And I don't want any more to do with her.'

'Dad said she seemed like a nice girl,' said Mum.

'She's not nice,' I said. 'She's weird. Totally weird.'

'That's what you said about Ruby when you met her first.'

'That's so not the same,' I protested. 'I admit Ruby's a small bit weird sometimes, but she's nice too.'

'And remember how hard you worked with Ruby and her mum? Remember how you helped them and how good that made you feel?'

She was right, but there was no way I was admitting that.

'That's all ancient history,' I said. 'Can't you understand, Mum? This is my summer holiday. I don't want to hang around with weirdos. I want to meet normal people, and have fun.'

Mum did the pouty thing with her mouth that showed me she was disappointed in me.

Just then there was a loud knock at the door.

'Try to be nice,' said Mum.

I almost weakened, but then I remembered that somewhere out there, Cathy and Lily, the cool girls, were waiting. I had to be tough.

'I'll get the door,' I said. 'I'm going to get rid of this girl once and for all.'

'Eva,' said Mum in a shocked voice, but I ignored her. I'd made up my mind.

I went to the door, practicing the line I'd thought of over breakfast.

Sorry, Kate, I'd love to come out with you, but I can't. I need to do family stuff – totally boring I know. In fact, it could go on for weeks – maybe even for the whole summer.

But when I opened the door, Kate was standing there, with one hand held out in front of her. She looked half-defiant, but also a bit lost and afraid.

'I found some wild strawberries,' she said. 'Do you want to share?'

I opened my mouth, but I found that I couldn't say the words I'd planned so carefully.

So I reached out and took one wild strawberry from Kate's still-outstretched hand. Feeling a bit like Snow White taking the rosy apple, I tasted the strawberry. The sudden sweetness took me totally by surprise.

'Wow! This is so yum!' I said.

Kate looked embarrassed. 'There are lots more and they're perfectly ripe,' she said. 'I can show you tomorrow, if you like.'

And even though I didn't want to be part of any tomorrow that included Kate, I found myself smiling, and saying, 'I'd like that thanks.'

Then we stood there and no one said anything, and it was totally, totally awkward.

After ages, and ages, Kate spoke again, 'Want to go for a walk?'

And even though I don't really 'do' walks, I just shrugged, and said, 'Whatever.'

Very strange.

✤   ♥   ♡

Kate led the way and I followed. Looked like we were walking to 'town' again.

'Do you think we'll meet the cool girls?' I said after a while.

Kate shook her head.

'I hope not,' she said, almost spitting the words out.

Then we walked some more without saying anything.

Just as we came near the village, Kate stopped walking.

'There they are,' she said. 'Look, over there,'

I looked where she was pointing, and saw two perfectly normal-looking girls sitting on a wall opposite one of the shops. I tried to flatten my curly hair, and then fixed my top.

'Come on,' I said to Kate. 'Introduce me.'

Kate took a step backwards.

'Trust me,' she said. 'You don't want to know them.'

I shook my head.

'You trust me; I *do* want to know them. Now introduce me, or I'm going home.'

'So go then,' said Kate defiantly, but when I turned, she caught my arm.

'Ok,' she said. 'I'll introduce you.'

I grinned. I *love* getting my own way.

'It's easy to remember who's who,' said Kate grumpily. 'Lily's the one with the dark hair, and she's mean, and Cathy's the one with the blonde hair, and she's really, really mean.'

'You can say what you like,' I said. 'But I'm not going to let you put me off.'

Kate didn't answer as she slouched over towards the two girls. I followed, trying not to look too happy.

The girls looked up as we approached, then one said something to the other and they both began to giggle. Kate's steps became even slower, but she kept walking.

Soon we were standing right next to the two girls, who were busy ignoring us.

I nudged Kate, but she didn't respond.

I gave a small cough, but the two girls just

continued admiring their nails. (I couldn't really blame them – they both had totally cool fake nails on.)

'We'd better go,' said Kate finally, pulling at my arm.

I dug my heels in. There was no way I was going without being introduced.

Eventually Kate gave a huge sigh.

'Cathy, Lily, this is Eva,' she said.

Lily looked up, and said 'hi' in a bored voice. Cathy just yawned.

I could feel my face going red. This was so unfair. Why were these girls acting like this? What did I ever do to them?

Suddenly I felt like I could see right into their minds. I knew what they must be thinking:

I was with Kate - Kate is totally uncool - I must be totally uncool too.

This was terrible. How could I make them understand the truth?

Before I could come up with a plan, Cathy

stood up.

'Time to go,' she said in a bored voice.

Then the other girl stood up, and they both walked off, sliding along in their totally cool flip-flops.

They couldn't leave.

How dare they leave?

I felt like running after them.

But what would I say?

So I watched as they slouched off, and then I turned back to Kate.

'See?' she said.

'I don't see anything,' I muttered. 'Now I've got to go. I think it's time for my tea, or my lunch or my nap or something.'

Kate just shrugged, so I walked off and left her.

In the end I couldn't resist looking back. She was still standing there, with her arms folded, looking sad and lost.

I felt sorry for her.

Of course I did.
But I felt much sorrier for me.

Chapter Eight

Next morning I got up early. It was a lovely sunny day, and I had a horrible feeling that Kate was going to call for me so that we could go to the beach together.

But if Kate called, I so didn't want to be there. I wanted to spend the day with Cathy and Lily, the girls I was sure were going to be my new best friends.

I spent ages getting ready. I wore some of the clothes I'd borrowed from Victoria and Ella. I put on the bracelet that Ruby had given me. I begged Mum to give me my hair-straightener back, and for once in her life she acted like a normal human being and gave it to me. I straightened my hair and immediately I felt like myself again. Then I set off for the village to meet my two new best friends.

It didn't take long to find them. They were sitting on the wall where I'd seen them the day before. I took a deep breath, fixed my collar and walked towards them.

They looked up as I approached. Cathy put her hand over her eyes to shield them from the sun. Then she whispered something to Lily and they both laughed.

Were they laughing at me?

How dare they laugh at me?

I thought of marching off, but my legs kept walking towards the two girls.

I got closer, and stood facing them for a second. No one said anything. The girls examined their nails again, and I kicked a pebble against the wall.

Then nothing happened.

I knew I had to be brave – my whole summer

holidays depended on it.

'Hi, I'm Eva,' I said, smiling brightly.

The girls looked up, but neither of them smiled back at me.

'We know,' said Lily.

'You're *Kate's* friend,' said Cathy.

'But I'm not,' I began. 'I just—' Cathy interrupted me. 'Kate's crazy, haven't you noticed?'

Lily continued. 'Crazy clothes, crazy hair, crazy girl.'

Then they both laughed.

'Kate smells bad,' said Cathy, holding her perfectly-shaped nose with her perfectly-manicured fingers.

'I know ....,' I began, but then I stopped myself.

Kate might be a bit different, but she wasn't crazy, and she *certainly* didn't smell bad. I hesitated, as all kinds of thoughts raced through my brain.

If I defended Kate, then these girls wouldn't like me.

And I so badly wanted them to like me.

But if I didn't defend Kate, then who would?

Cathy spoke again. 'Kate is the biggest loser in the whole wide world,' she said.

And that's when I made up my mind.

'I think Kate's great,' I said.

Then I turned and walked away.

I'd only gone a few metres when I had a horrible thought. I'd just kissed goodbye to my dream of making cool friends on this holiday. If I didn't do something quickly, I wouldn't see anyone cool until I got to see Victoria and Ella again, and that could be weeks away.

I turned around, ready to tell Cathy and Lily that I'd just been joking – that I agreed with them about Kate. I even started to say it.

'I was just ……,' I began.

But Cathy and Lily weren't listening. They were pointing at me and laughing, and I knew that there was no going back.

I'm not stupid.

I knew that if Cathy and Lily were always so mean, then they weren't worth being friends with.

Still though, I had a sick, horrible feeling in my stomach as I slowly walked away.

✦ ☼ ✿

When I got home, Mum and Joey were in the kitchen.

'Did you have a nice walk?' asked Mum.

I shook my head.

'No,' I said. 'It was totally awful. Walks are never much fun, but that was the worst walk of my whole life.'

And then, because I had nothing left to lose, I told her the whole story.

When I was finished, Mum came over and hugged me.

'That was brave of you, Eva,' she said. 'I'm

very proud of you.'

I tried to smile. Making Mum proud was a nice feeling, but could it ever make up for having no cool friends?

'So is Kate your new best friend now?' asked Joey, like he could read my mind.

Before I could answer, he continued. 'I hope she is, because she called over when you were out, and your mum invited her to come for lunch.'

Chapter Nine

At one o'clock there was a knock on the door.

For one small second, I allowed myself to hope that it might be Cathy and Lily. Maybe they wanted to tell me they'd only been joking when they'd said those mean things about Kate, and that they really wanted to be friends with me.

But my small hope faded as Joey raced over to answer the door. Seconds later, Kate came into the room. She was still wearing the boys' tracksuit and runners, but her hair was neatly combed, and her face was red and shiny, like she'd just finished washing it.

She looked embarrassed as she held a bunch of battered wild flowers towards Mum.

'I brought you these,' she said.

Mum took them and held them to her nose.

'Thank you very– eeeeek,' she screeched, dropping the flowers to the floor.

Now Kate looked even more embarrassed.

Joey ran over to investigate.

'Cool!' he said. 'It's an earwig. But I don't think Paula likes earwigs all that much.'

I giggled. Mum's absolutely terrified of earwigs. Dad stepped forward with a rolled-up newspaper.

'Where is it?' he asked. 'I'll finish it off.'

'No!' said Kate loudly, and we all stared at her.

'No,' she said more softly. 'Don't kill it. I'll catch it and take it outside.'

Before anyone could argue, Kate had scooped up the tiny creature and put it gently on the grass beside the front door.

Mum recovered herself.

'Sorry, Kate,' she said. 'They're really lovely flowers, and it was kind of you to bring them. Pick them up please Joey, and put them ...... put them in a vase in the other room.'

Joey did what he was told, and then we all sat down for our lunch.

Dad served up the food, and we started to eat. Apart from the scraping of our knives and forks, there was a long awkward silence around the table.

Even Joey was unusually quiet.

'Do you like school, Kate?' asked Mum after a while.

What kind of a question was that?

Better than any I could think of.

Kate's mouth was full of food, and she chewed frantically before she could answer. 'Not really,' she said, and then there was another long silence.

Mum and Dad kept trying to break the silence, but after a few sentences, the conversation always came to a sudden halt. It was turning into the longest lunch of my life.

Then Joey managed to liven things up.

'Who do you live with?' he asked Kate.

I stopped eating so I could listen carefully. I really wanted to know the answer to that question. Kate didn't talk a whole lot, and she *never* talked about her family. And any time I asked her a question she avoided it or half-answered it with a single word. Now, with Mum and Dad listening, what was she going to say?

'I live with my granny,' she said after a while.

'Your granny?' repeated Mum.

Kate was going red.

'Yes, but I call her Martha.'

'Why do you call her that?' asked Joey.

Kate giggled.

'Because it's her name.'

Everyone laughed then, except for Joey who hates it when he thinks people are laughing at him.

'So where are your mum and dad?' he said

crossly. 'Why don't you live with *them*?'

'Joey!' said Mum, but she didn't say any more. I figured she was as curious as I was.

'I don't remember my mum,' began Kate. 'She went away when I was very small.'

'Where did she go?' asked Joey.

Kate shrugged.

'Dublin, I think. No one really knows for sure.'

'And did she come back?' asked Joey.

Kate shook her head.

Mum patted her arm.

'I'm sorry to hear that.'

Kate shrugged again.

'That's OK. Martha says my mum wasn't cut out to be a mother, and that I'm probably better off without her.'

I tried to get my head around what she was saying. My mum can be a total pain sometimes, but I couldn't imagine what life would be like if she just packed up and walked away.

'That's awful,' I said in the end.

Kate spoke as if she couldn't get the words out fast enough.

'It didn't matter so much, not having Mum around, because I had Dad – and we were very happy. Dad was really fun. We did loads of things together. We went on long walks all over the place. He taught me all about plants and birds and stuff. He showed me where to find the best wild strawberries and mushrooms. He used to pack picnics, and we'd go off for the whole day, just the two of us. We had this special place where no one else went. We called it the Island of Dreams. There was a big tree there. Sometimes I used to climb right to the top. Sometimes we'd bring a rug and we'd sit in the shade of the tree for hours, and Dad used to make up these wild stories about pirates and highwaymen and stuff.'

By now everyone had stopped eating. Joey was actually holding a forkful of food in the air, but was too spellbound to put it into his mouth.

OK, so maybe sitting under a tree, with my dad telling fairy stories wasn't my idea of a fun day out, but the way Kate told it, it seemed like something magical.

Kate went on talking, almost like it was a dream, and she was still part of it.

'Sometimes, during the holidays, whole days went by, and we didn't see anyone else. Sometimes we even camped up in the Island of Dreams. We used to put up this tiny tent, and we'd lie there with the tent-flaps open, so we could watch the stars. Dad knew all about the stars – he knew the names of loads of them. In the morning we'd watch the sun come up, and it was just like magic, watching the start of a whole new day. And when we got home, Martha would pretend to be cross, but she wasn't really. And she'd sit us up at the big kitchen table and she'd make us pancakes, and then the next day we'd do it all over again.'

Kate stopped talking, and there was another silence.

Then Joey asked the question I hadn't been brave enough for.

'Then what happened?'

The dreamy look vanished from Kate's face, like someone had pressed the 'erase' button.

'Then something terrible happened,' she said.

'What?' persisted Joey.

It was ages before Kate answered, and when she did so, it was in a voice so soft that we all had to lean forward so we could hear her properly. Joey's forkful of food was nearly touching his nose, but he didn't seem to notice.

'You see…' began Kate.

She stopped, looked around the table at all of us, and then started again in an even quieter voice – almost a whisper.

'My dad died,' she said.

I gasped.

Mum and Dad looked at each other.

Joey grinned. 'Cool,' he said. 'How did that happen?'

I kicked him under the table, and Dad said 'Joey,' in a real fierce voice, but Kate just shrugged. 'It's OK,' she said. 'I don't mind. I'm used to it by now.'

Then in the same soft, whispery voice, she finished her story.

'It was a lovely sunny day, the kind of day you never want to end. Dad and I had been to the Island of Dreams, and we were on our way home. Dad was carrying the rug, and I was carrying the picnic basket. I always carried the basket on the way home, because it was lighter then. Dad used to tease me about that. And when we got to the junction at the top of the hill, there was this injured bird, right in the middle of the road. It was flapping its wings madly, but no matter how hard it flapped, it couldn't fly away. And Dad loved all creatures, especially birds, and he could never ever just

leave it alone to die. So he stepped out to try to help it, but he didn't see the truck that was coming around the corner. He............'
Kate stopped talking, but even Joey was smart enough to figure out what happened next.

There was a very long silence.

I looked desperately at Mum and Dad. They were the grown-ups, and they should know what to say next. For once in her life, though, Mum was speechless. She just patted Kate's hand. I could see by Kate's face that this made her feel uncomfortable, and that she was resisting the urge to pull her hand away.

I felt sorry for Kate.

I felt sorry for Mum.

I felt sorry for all of us.

At last, Dad cleared his throat, and I breathed a sigh of relief. Then he spoke in a strange, bright voice.

'Now then,' he said. 'Who's ready for more pasta?'

Chapter Ten

After lunch, I started to clear off the table, but Mum pushed me away.

'I'll do that,' she said. 'You and Kate go off outside.'

Usually I'm happy when I don't have to help out with jobs, but right then, clearing the table seemed a lot easier than trying to think of something to say to Kate.

Kate and I went outside and sat on the wall beside our house. It was a lovely sunny day. But even that made me feel bad. Did every sunny day remind Kate of the day her dad died?

'Er ... I'm really sorry about ... you know ... what happened to your dad,' I said in the end.

'That's OK,' she said. 'It was ages ago. Like I said to Joey – I'm used to it now.'

I didn't answer. How could *anyone* get used to something like that? I get mad with my dad sometimes, but never so mad that I'd like to see him walk out in front of a huge truck.

After ages, Kate spoke again. 'You and me, we're friends now, right?'

At first I didn't answer. My friends were the kind of girls who wore cool clothes, and talked about music and films and stuff, not strange, wild girls with short hair and boys' clothes, who talked about stars and butterflies and mushrooms.

But how could I say that to Kate?

Especially now?

So I shrugged and said. 'Sure. We're friends.'

I was embarrassed at how happy Kate was when I said this. It was almost like I'd given her a present.

She smiled at me, and I had a horrible feeling

that I'd never seen her smile before. She looked almost pretty when she smiled – with perfect white teeth, and sparkly eyes. I thought about telling her that she should smile more often, but I stopped myself. After her sad life, she probably only allowed herself one or two smiles a year.

'Since we're friends,' she said. 'Do you want me to show you the Island of Dreams?'

'Show me what?' I asked, pretending not to understand.

'The Island of Dreams. The special place I used to go to with my dad.'

I gulped.

I *so* didn't want to go there.

How creepy was it to be hanging out in a place that reminded my poor, weird friend of her dead father?

But how could I possibly say no?

✮ ♥ ♡

It wasn't far – just about ten minutes walk from

our house. It seemed like a long way though, because for the last few hundred metres, Kate insisted on walking behind me with her hands over my eyes. I felt a bit dizzy, and once I scraped my leg on a wall, but I couldn't complain. Now that I knew about Kate's mum and dad, how could I give her a hard time over anything?

As we got closer though, I began to get a bit excited. The Island of Dreams sounded totally cool – like a place from a fantasy story.

And when Kate said, 'I'm so happy to be bringing you here. At last you'll be able to meet Jeremy,' I got very, very excited.

Who was Jeremy, and why hadn't Kate mentioned him before?

I began to picture a totally cool boy, with tanned skin and sun-bleached hair. Maybe he'd have an amazing Californian or Australian accent.

This could be the start of the perfect holiday.

At last we were there.

Kate took her hands from my eyes with a big flourish.

'Ta da!' she said, as if I was going to open my eyes and see something like the fairy castle in Disneyland or a shopping centre full of all my favourite shops.

I opened my eyes, and rubbed them until I could see properly. Then I rubbed them again, just in case I was missing something.

We were standing in a field – a plain old field just like hundreds of others all around us.

'Well?' said Kate. 'What do you think?'

What I thought was that maybe this whole thing was a big joke, but I didn't like to say this – just in case.

'Er …,' I began.

Kate grinned. 'I know. You're speechless. That's OK. I know how you feel.'

I smiled weakly.

'Look around you,' commanded Kate.

I did as she said.

'What do you see?'

Nothing?

'Well?' she asked.

'This isn't an island,' I said in the end.

Kate shrugged.

'I know it's not a *real* island, but Dad used to say that to us it was as good as an island. Once we were here, the rest of the world seemed very far away.'

'The rest of the world' – that reminded me.

'Where's Jeremy?' I asked.

'Right over there,' she said, pointing.

I looked but couldn't see anyone.

Was he hiding behind the tree?

I walked around the tree but there was no-one there. Then I looked up into the branches, not sure I wanted to see anyone up there.

The cool, blond boy of my imagination was

starting to turn into a hunched wild thing with dirty, matted hair, who could only communicate with grunts and gestures.

'I don't see him,' I said in the end.

Kate laughed.

'You're looking right at him,' she said.

Now I felt cross. Clearly there was no one there. What kind of stupid game did she think she was playing?

Surely she was too old to have an imaginary friend?

'Jeremy is the tree,' she said.

I'd have laughed if I hadn't been so shocked.

I'm just a normal girl.

This shouldn't be happening to me.

What had gone so wrong in my life that I was hanging around with a mad girl who gave boys' names to trees?

Kate seemed to be waiting for some kind of response from me.

'Er ... why do you call the tree Jeremy?' I said

in the end.

Kate looked concerned.

'What's wrong? Don't you think Jeremy is a good name? You and I could think of a new one if you like. What about Walter …or … Harry?'

I opened my mouth, but no sound came out.

Kate put her head in her hands.

'I shouldn't have told you about Jeremy,' she said. 'Now you think I'm an idiot.'

I couldn't deny this, so I said nothing.

'I know it's crazy calling trees names,' she said. 'Dad did it when I was small, to make me laugh. And it kind of became a habit. And now I'm used to it, so I just keep doing it. You don't mind, do you?'

I couldn't answer her, so she continued.

'I bet you did stuff like that when you were small. I bet you gave names to things that really shouldn't have names.'

I suddenly thought of Billy Blankie, the scrap of blue fleece that I couldn't sleep without until

I was about seven.

Kate stared at me, almost like she could read my mind.

'So you don't think I'm an idiot?' she asked.

I pushed away the picture of Billy Blankie, who was still buried at the bottom of a drawer in my bedroom at home.

'Maybe it's just me,' I said, avoiding her question. 'But I'm really not comfortable calling trees by names. I'll just keep calling it a tree, if that's OK by you.'

Kate patted the tree trunk.

'That's no problem. I'm sure Jeremy won't mind – since you're my friend.'

I wondered if she was joking, but her serious face gave me no clue.

'Jeremy really is special, you know,' she said.

'How?' I said, wondering what kind of mad thing she was going to come up with next.

'Can he talk, or dance or juggle lemons while singing the national anthem?'

Kate ignored my sarcastic tone.

'He's the only big tree for miles around. Trees don't grow very well up here – it's too windy, but Jeremy survived. He's been here for more than a hundred years – it's like magic.'

I looked around me, and realised that she was right. All the other trees I could see were scrawny, and bent over like they were cowering in front of the wind.

'Let's climb Jeremy,' said Kate suddenly.

I giggled, suddenly seeing the funny side of this bizarre conversation.

'Only if you think it won't hurt him.' Kate laughed too, and before I could say another word, she was clinging on to the first branch like a monkey.

I like climbing trees, so I followed her, and soon we were both balancing on a broad branch halfway up the very tall tree. Kate moved to one side.

'Here,' she said. 'You can have the best place

since it's your first time here.'

I edged past her, and leaned against the trunk of the tree. A soft breeze was rustling the leaves, and in the distance I could see the sea, sparkling like someone had sprinkled body glitter all over it.

I closed my eyes. The tree was swaying ever so slightly, and the rustling leaves were calming – almost like a lullaby.

When I opened my eyes again, Kate had stretched herself along a flat part of the branch, and was gazing out to sea. All at once, I felt like maybe she was right. There *was* something magical about this place.

I patted the branch I was sitting on. 'You're OK, Jeremy,' I said, and Kate gave a small smile.

After a while Kate stirred. 'Race you to the big hedge at the far side of that field,' she said, pointing. Then she scrambled down the tree and began to run. I climbed down after her, and raced through the long grass, laughing as I ran.

We pushed our way through two small hedges, crossed a field and then galloped up a steep hill.

We reached the big hedge together, and threw ourselves down on to the grass, too breathless to talk. Even though I'm *much* too old for that kind of stuff, it was totally the most fun thing I'd done in ages.

Chapter Eleven

When I got home, Mum was in the kitchen. I ran over and hugged her.

'What was that for?' she asked when I finally let her go.

'For not running away when I was a baby,' I said, feeling a bit stupid as the words came out.

Mum hugged me again, and when she let me go I could see tears in her eyes.

'That poor girl,' she said. 'I don't think I've ever heard anything so sad.'

I shook my head.

'Me neither.'

'Are you going to see her tomorrow?' asked Mum.

I nodded.

'Yeah. She said she'll call over in the morning.'

Mum smiled at me.

'That's good. It sounds like the poor thing needs a friend. It was nice of you to defend her against those other two girls this morning.'

'Thanks, but I really wanted to be friends with *them*. Cathy and Lily seem much more like my type. They're cool and fashionable, and I bet they like the same kind of stuff as I do.'

'I understand where you're coming from,' said Mum. 'Remember though, Victoria and Ella are cool and fashionable, but they're also nice girls. This Cathy and Lily sound very mean to me. Better to stay well away from them.'

Then Mum went and rooted around in her handbag.

'You showed great maturity today, Eva,' she said. 'So I think it's time you got this back.' As she spoke, she pulled out my phone.

I raced over and took it from her. I turned

it over and over in my hands like it was a precious jewel. Then I pressed the 'on' button and watched as the screen lit up. Just as I was admiring my totally cool screensaver, the phone rang.

I answered the call and held the phone to my ear.

'About time.'

It was Victoria, and even though it was only a few days since we'd hugged goodbye, it felt like hundreds of years had passed since then.

'I've been trying to call you for ages,' Victoria continued. 'Did your parents confiscate your phone again?'

'Yes,' I replied.

'What did you do this time?' she asked.

I sighed.

'It's kind of a long story.'

'You mean your mum's listening.'

I giggled.

'Exactly.'

Then I waved to Mum and walked out into the garden so Victoria and I could talk in peace.

Victoria laughed when I told her about the 'kidnapped' sign, and then she told me about the fun stuff she'd been doing since I had left.

'So what have you been doing besides wasting police time?' she asked after a while. 'How are the holidays going?'

I hesitated.

I wanted to tell her about Kate, but didn't know how, without making Kate sound totally weird.

'It's kind of boring,' I said, 'I haven't really made any friends yet.'

'Poor you,' she said, not sounding as sympathetic as I had hoped.

Then she said, 'But you haven't asked why I'm ringing.'

'Because I'm one of your best friends and you miss me and wanted to talk to me?'

She laughed. 'That too, but it's mostly because

my Mum is going to visit an old school-friend tomorrow afternoon.'

'And I care about that because?' I said in the most bored voice I could manage.

'Because Mum's friend lives a few miles from where you are now, and Mum said that she'll bring me with her, and I can hang out with you for a few hours until she has to go back again!'

I squealed and jumped up and down. I couldn't believe it. I was going to see my friend. For the first time in days, I was going to see a real, live, normal friend.

Victoria laughed again. 'Get over yourself,' she said. 'Or else I won't come. Now my mum wants to talk to your mum so we can get directions to your place. And I'll ring you tomorrow to tell you what time I'll be there.'

I raced inside, gave the phone to Mum and minutes later it was all settled. I threw myself on to a couch and gave a big sigh of happiness.

Everything was perfect.

And then I had a horrible thought.

What was I going to do about Kate?

✸   ❤   ♡

In the end, I was so desperate I decided to ask Mum for advice. She didn't think it was a big deal.

'Kate calls over, Victoria arrives, and you all hang out together for a few hours. I'm afraid I don't see the problem,' she said.

I felt like stamping my foot but didn't dare. I didn't want to give Mum a reason to take my phone back again.

'You just don't *get* it,' I said. 'Kate is totally different to Victoria. She wouldn't like Victoria, and Victoria wouldn't like her.'

Mum just smiled. 'They both seem to like you,' she said.

Now I risked a small stamp of my foot. 'That's *so* not the point. It just wouldn't work. It would be a total disaster. It would ruin my only day with Victoria. It would ruin my holiday. It would ruin my whole life.'

Mum patted my shoulder. 'I don't think it's as serious as all that,' she said. 'If you want my opinion—'

'I don't,' I said crossly, but Mum ignored me and continued, 'If you want my opinion, I think you should trust your friends to get on with each other.'

'But….'

'Remember when you first met Ruby?' continued Mum. 'She was a bit of a loner, but in the end she got on fine with all your other friends.'

'That's different,' I said.

'How?'

'It just is.'

Mum sighed. 'Well then, if you're going to be like that, you'd better go and explain to Kate. You can't have her come over here tomorrow and not invite her in. That would be too cruel.

Think of something nice to say to her, and tell her you'll see her the day after tomorrow. Now off you go, it's nearly time for tea.'

Chapter Twelve

Typical Mum, she makes everything sound so easy, but as I walked slowly towards Kate's house, I knew this wasn't going to be quite as simple as it seemed.

How was I going to explain to Kate?

Do you think you could sort of vanish from my life for twenty-four hours?

You're not as weird as I thought you were at first, but you're still too weird to meet my real friend.

Let's play hide-and seek. You hide and I'll look for you – the day after tomorrow.

No matter how I tried, I couldn't think of a nice way to say what I needed to say. Kate wasn't stupid, and I knew it would be very easy to hurt her feelings.

Much too soon, I was at the top of the laneway leading to Kate's house. I'd never been here before. Kate always called for me, and she had never invited me to her place. Now I thought I could see why. The laneway was all overgrown, with barely space for one person to pass through. Long thorny branches grabbed at my clothes, like they were trying to hold me back.

Did they know something I didn't?

At the top of the lane was a small cottage that might once have been white, but was now a dull grey colour. The roof was covered with gross slimy green stuff. The paint on the front door was faded and peeling, and the grass in front looked like it hadn't been cut in months.

Poor Kate. Having no mum or dad was horrible enough, but living in a dump like this made things even worse.

(OK, so right now, I was living in a dump not

much better than this, but that was just because of one of my mum's crazy ideas. Back home, in my real life, our clean, not-falling-down house was waiting for us.)

Just as I was trying to find the courage to knock on the door, Kate appeared at the side of the house. She jumped when she saw me, then ran towards me.

'What are you doing here?' she hissed.

'I … I …,' I began.

'You shouldn't come here,' said Kate. 'You should *never* come here.'

As she spoke, she took my arm and dragged me back towards my own house. I didn't resist. Kate suddenly seemed fierce and frightening, and there was no way I was doing anything that might make her even worse.

As we got farther way from her house, Kate seemed to relax a bit. She let go of my arm. We stopped walking and stood staring at each other. I rubbed my arm, wondering if Kate's fingers were going to be forever imprinted on my skin.

'Sorry, Eva,' she said after a while. 'It's just ... it's just ... well it's just that you kind of gave me a fright ... and Martha doesn't like visitors. Since Dad ...... since Dad ......, well, no one ever calls, and Martha's got used to it. She likes it that way. She's kind of a recluse.'

'But what about you?' I protested. 'That's not fair on you. You're not a recluse. Why do you have to live like that?'

'You don't have to worry about me. I'm tough.'

But something in the way she said it, made me realise that, despite her fierce look, she wasn't tough at all.

'Anyway,' said Kate brightly. 'Enough about me. What do you want? Why were you calling for me?'

I gulped.

The way Kate had reacted had made me forget all about why I was there, but now I was more sure than ever that I had to keep her away from my real friend.

'Er … I came to say that my friend, Victoria, is coming for the afternoon tomorrow.'

Kate grinned. 'That's great news. You probably miss her. We can show her the Island of Dreams if you like. I don't mind sharing it as long as she's a friend of yours. We won't mention Jeremy, though, if you think she won't get it. And we can show her where the wild strawberries grow – but you have to make her promise not to tell anyone.' Kate looked up and saw my face.

'Oh,' she said. 'I've got this wrong, haven't I?'

I nodded slowly.

'Don't worry, Eva,' she said. 'I understand.'

I was beginning to feel really happy, before she continued.

'I guess your friend isn't into that kind of thing. That's OK, though, there's loads of other stuff we can do. We could go to the beach, or we could ……'

'Er, Kate ……,' I began.

She looked up again and her smile vanished.

'You don't want me hanging around while your friend is here, do you?' she said.

'I.......' I began, but couldn't think how to go on.

'It's OK,' she said. 'I know how you feel. You're ashamed of me.'

'It's not like that,' I protested, even though she was right. I felt awful, as a mixture of guilt and relief washed over me.

'I don't mind,' said Kate. 'I understand. I'd probably do the same if I were you. Anyway, I'm very busy tomorrow. Martha wants me to do some jobs for her. Even if you wanted to spend time with me, I probably wouldn't be able to.'

I knew she was lying, but I didn't argue.

Kate gave a sad smile. 'Have a nice day with your friend.'

I wondered if my guilty conscience would let me enjoy a single second of my time with Victoria.

'We can hang out the day after tomorrow, if you like,' I said, feeling like a snake.

'That sounds good. I'll call for you in the morning, OK?'

I nodded, and Kate walked slowly away.

I watched her go.

She'd solved my problem for me, but why did I feel like this was the meanest thing I'd ever done in my entire life?

Chapter Thirteen

I got up early the next morning, and it seemed like ages before Victoria arrived. I was totally bored. I wished I could hang out with Kate for a while, but I knew that wasn't a good idea.

Mum persuaded me to play Monopoly with Joey. It was so boring that I kept robbing the bank to give him extra money so that he'd win and put me out of my misery. He caught me though, and insisted that we go back and start the whole thing again. I wondered for the hundredth time why I'd ever dreamed of having a little brother or sister.

Every few minutes, I jumped up and looked

out the window.

Why wasn't Victoria here?

I texted her heaps of times, but she never replied.

Why didn't she ring me?

Had something more exciting come up, and had she changed her mind about coming to visit me?

At last I heard the sound of a car and I raced out to greet my friend.

'Omigod! You're here at last,' I said.

Victoria's mum laughed.

'It's only been a few days,' she said, but Victoria and I were too busy hugging to answer her.

Victoria's mum arranged to be back at five, and then she set off for her friend's house.

Victoria followed me inside. She gazed around the room.

'I know,' I said. 'It's a dump. You'll get used to it after a while.'

She shook her head. 'It's not a dump. It's … quaint, and kind of cute.'

I tried to see it through her eyes, but failed.

'Why didn't you ring me this morning like you said you would?' I asked.

Victoria made a face. 'I couldn't. My phone had an accident.'

I tried unsuccessfully not to giggle. Victoria's phone is always having accidents.

'What happened this time?'

'Er …it fell down the toilet.'

This time I didn't even try to hide the giggles. Victoria giggled too.

'It's not really funny though. It probably can't be fixed, and Mum won't buy me a new one until September. She says I'm too careless.'

'Poor you,' I said. 'But look on the bright side, at least you're not stuck in a weird dump like this for the summer.'

'Speaking of weird,' said Victoria. 'We passed a girl on the road, just before we got here, and she was acting really weird.'

'Weird how?' I asked, not sure that I wanted to hear the answer.

'It looked like she was crawling through the hedge or something,' said Victoria.

'That's …………..,' began Joey, who always seemed to be around when I didn't want him.

'Hey,' said Victoria. 'You must be Joey.'

Joey gave her his best gap-toothed smile.

'So cute,' said Victoria smiling back.

I was starting to agree with her, when he went on talking.

'That girl you saw is Eva's new best friend, Kate,' he said. 'She's really funny. She doesn't mind picking up earwigs or anything. She—'

I couldn't take any more. I picked up a magazine, and lightly whacked Joey on the head with it. Then I raced out the door before he could go crying to Mum and Dad.

I ran down the road to safety, with Victoria laughing and running after me.

There was no sign of Kate, but unfortunately Victoria hadn't forgotten about her.

'Is that girl we saw really your friend?' she asked. 'If you don't mind me saying it, she didn't exactly look like your type.'

I hesitated. I knew I should be loyal to Kate, but I wasn't brave enough. So I shook my head.

'No. She's not my friend. She's just a girl who lives around here. Joey only made that friend stuff up to annoy me.'

'Good,' sighed Victoria. 'We wouldn't want you going all weird on us. Now what's there to do in this place?'

It didn't take long to tell her. My favourite place was The Island of Dreams, but I could hardly take Victoria there. For one thing, Kate might show up. It wasn't just that, though. I'd betrayed Kate enough already, but taking my friend to her favourite place without her would have been totally mean.

So we decided to walk to the beach.

As usual, Cathy and Lily were sitting on the wall opposite the shop. It was almost like they were living statues, part of the scenery.

'Who are those two girls over there?' asked Victoria. 'Do you know them?'

Yes, but they think I'm weird just like my friend Kate.

'Not really,' I said.

'So let's get to know them,' said Victoria, who can make friends with anyone.

Maybe she was right. If Cathy and Lily saw me with my real friend, my cool friend, maybe they'd forget that Kate was my friend too. Maybe they'd like me. Maybe I was going to have a half-way normal summer after all.

As we walked towards Cathy and Lily, I fixed my hair and straightened my top.

Cathy and Lily gave us their usual bored looks as we came close.

'Hi, Kate's friend,' said Cathy.

Victoria gave me a funny look, before Cathy

continued. 'Where's Kate today? Digging potatoes? Eating worms? Swinging out of trees?'

I could feel my face going red. I should have known that this was a stupid idea.

And to make things even worse, I couldn't think of a single smart thing to say back to Cathy.

'Come on,' I said to Victoria, pulling her by her arm. 'Let's hurry, I want to show you the beach before the tide comes in.'

Victoria followed me to the beach, but as soon as we got there, she made me stop and she stared me in the face.

'What's going on, Eva?' she asked.

I took a step backwards. Victoria can be very intimidating when she wants to.

Then she continued, 'Why are those girls being so mean? Why is everyone saying that Kate is your friend, even though you deny it?' Now Victoria folded her arms, and put on her crossest face. 'Tell me, Eva,' she said.

I shrugged. 'There's nothing to tell. This place is full of weirdos. Didn't I say that already? Now we only have a few hours, so let's start enjoying ourselves.'

✮ ♥ ♡

We had a totally fun day, and when Victoria's mum came to pick her up, I felt like crying.

I gave Victoria one last hug, and then she climbed in to the front of her mum's car and slammed the door.

I waved and tried to smile as they drove off. I felt like Victoria was abandoning me. Without her, Kate was the closest I had to a friend.

But how could someone be your friend if you were half-afraid of them?

It just wasn't fair.

Summer wasn't supposed to be like this.

✮ ♥ ♡

Kate called over first thing the next morning.

'Did you have a nice time with your friend?' she asked.

I went red. 'I'm sorry about … well you know … I'm sorry,' I said.

Kate smiled. 'That's OK.'

She seemed so nice, and so forgiving, that for one second I felt like hugging her. Then I remembered that she wasn't really a huggy kind of girl, so I just smiled back, and we set off for another day at the beach.

Chapter Fourteen

The next day, Kate and I were lying on the grass in the Island of Dreams. We were watching the clouds drifting overhead, and Kate was inventing stories about where they were going to end up.

'Don't you ever wish that you could know what's going to happen in the future?' she asked suddenly.

'No,' I said quickly, before I remembered. 'Actually once I did,' I said. 'I even went to see a fortune-teller.'

Kate rolled over and lay on her stomach. She rested her chin on her hands and stared at me.

'Tell me,' she said.

'I was going through a really hard time,' I said. 'Dad had lost his job, and we'd had to move to a much smaller house. I had to leave the school I loved and go to one where I didn't know anybody. My life was a total disaster.'

Kate said nothing, but suddenly I realised that, compared to Kate's life, mine had never been even close to being disastrous.

'At the time, my life *seemed* like a total disaster,' I corrected myself.

'And?'

'And I went to see a fortune-teller, Madame Margarita. And she told me that if I helped people, my life would get better.'

'You needed a fortune-teller to tell you that?'

I smiled. 'I was very mixed-up at the time. So I spent months helping people, and in the end it turned out that Madam Margarita was right. Things did start to get better.'

'I'm glad,' said Kate, and I knew that she meant it.

'But the funniest thing is, there was a girl in my class called Ruby, and I helped her the most. So one day she invited me over to her place and it turned out that Madam Margarita was her mum!'

'No way!'

'Yes way. Except she wasn't a real fortune-teller at all. She was just an ordinary woman called Maggie.'

'That's totally amazing,' said Kate. I could tell by her face that she was really interested.

I had a funny feeling that if I'd been friends with Cathy and Lily, I never could have told them this story – they'd have laughed or teased me about being so stupid.

I knew from the start that Kate was different, but now I realised that she was different in a nice way.

✦　♥　♡

The next few weeks went by very quickly. Kate

and I spent every day together. She didn't know much about cool stuff like clothes or music, but she knew loads about plants and birds, and she knew all kinds of strange places to explore.

Kate didn't mention her mum or dad any more, and neither did I. That whole thing was much too embarrassing for me. I was afraid of saying the wrong thing, so I decided it would be easier to say nothing at all.

I couldn't say that I was *loving* my time in the country, but I was sort of getting used to it. Victoria still had no phone, and Ella was helping her dad run his summer camp on a remote island that had no mobile phone coverage. Ruby was too busy swimming to have time to text me. I was cut off from the outside world, and in some ways, it was almost like my old life didn't exist. And then one day, everything changed.

Chapter Fifteen

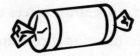

Kate called early that morning, as usual. (Since that first day, I hadn't dared to go near her house again.)

'I'm going out,' I called, but Mum raced after me.

'You're not going anywhere until you tidy your room,' she said. 'It's like a pig-sty.'

'How do you know?' I asked. 'Have you been in a pig-sty recently?'

I thought that was quite funny, but it didn't help me much. It just made Mum crosser.

I made a face at Kate who was standing watching the scene. That made me feel guilty – she probably wished she had a mum to have rows with.

'You go ahead,' I said. 'I might be a while.'

Kate grinned. 'OK. See you in the Island of Dreams when you're finished.'

Ten minutes later, I'd finished tidying my room. (Well, I'd finished stuffing everything under my bed.) I called good-bye to Mum and Dad and Joey, and set off for the field.

As I strolled along, I could hear a robin and a sparrow singing in the hedge. (Clearly I was spending too much time with Kate, if I actually knew what robins and sparrows sounded like.)

I walked around a bend to find Kate racing towards me. Her tracksuit was torn, her knee was bleeding, and she was crying so much I couldn't hear what she was trying to say. Eventually she caught her breath and got some real words out.

'There's a ... man ...... a big man ... with a ...... with a ... he's got a ... chain ... saw and he ...'

Now it was my turn to panic. This was like

something from a horror movie. I grabbed Kate's arm and tried to pull her down the hill.

'So why are we hanging around?' I gasped. 'Let's get out of here … quickly! Let's get back to my place. Come on! Run! Someone needs to call the police.'

Kate shook her head.

'You don't understand. The man isn't trying to hurt me.'

'But what happened to your leg? And why are you crying?'

Kate looked at her leg, like she'd just noticed that it was bleeding.

'That's nothing. I fell when I was running down the hill. And I'm crying because …' at that she started to cry again. 'I'm crying because … because … the man … is trying to cut … he's trying to cut down …… Jeremy.'

I was glad to know that our lives weren't in immediate danger, but this was still terrible news.

'He can't do that,' I said.

'But he is.'

Now I turned around and tried to pull her back up the hill.

'We've got to stop him,' I said.

Kate shook her head.

'How? He's got a chainsaw, and he says he's got orders from the man who owns the tree. There's nothing we can do.'

I made a face.

'There's *always* something you can do. Now are you coming with me or not?'

Kate didn't answer, but she followed me back up the hill to the field.

There was a jeep parked in the laneway, and there were three men in the field. They'd put long spike things into the ground all around Jeremy, and they'd looped yellow tape from one spike to the other, making a low fence. The tape was official-looking, and said stuff like *Danger* and *Tree-felling* and *Keep Out*. One of the men was busy pouring petrol into the tank of a huge chainsaw.

'What are you doing?' I shouted.

The man stopped what he was doing and stared at me.

'Guess,' he said.

Great. An adult who thought he was smart.

'I'm a bit too big for guessing games,' I said.

The man shrugged. 'I'll tell you, then. We're cutting down this tree – not that it's any of your business.'

'But you can't do that,' I said.

'Actually we can,' said the man. 'And I told your friend that already.' As he spoke, he pulled a cord and the chainsaw engine started with a huge roar.

'Now run along out of here,' he shouted. 'Tree-cutting is a dangerous business, and we don't want anyone getting hurt.'

I turned to look at Kate. She was standing still – almost like she'd been turned to stone.

She was pale, and tears were streaming down her face.

I knew I had to do something.

But what on earth *could* I do?

Kate was too shocked to be any use, and there was no time for me to run and get Mum or Dad or anyone else.

I was on my own.

And how could one girl be a match for three men and a chainsaw?

'Hey, what's that?' I said suddenly, pointing towards the sea.

As the three men turned to look, I ducked under the yellow tape, and ran over and stood with my back to Jeremy. After a second, Kate followed me, and we stood there, giving Jeremy a kind of backwards hug.

The man flicked a switch, and the chainsaw stopped its ferocious noise. He laid it on the grass and walked over to us. The other two men came and stood next to him, like he needed to be protected from Kate and me.

The man with the chainsaw spoke. 'I suppose you think you're very clever,' he said.

I didn't answer, and Kate gave a sniffly sob.

'Look kids,' he said in a gentler voice. 'I don't know what's going on here, but it's time for you to stop this messing about. We've got a job to do, and you're getting in the way. Now run along and play, and let us get on with what we're paid to do.'

Suddenly Kate spoke. Her voice was quiet, but fierce.

'I won't allow you to hurt Jeremy.'

The man sighed. 'Who's Jeremy, when he's at home?'

'Jeremy is the tree,' said Kate.

The man was foolish enough to laugh, but he didn't laugh for long. Kate stepped forward and glared at him so hard that he actually took a step backwards. Then he recovered himself.

'That's enough nonsense, girls,' he said. 'Now run along. Please.'

We didn't move.

For a few minutes nothing much happened.

The wind rustled the branches over our head.

A cow in the next field mooed loudly.

Kate and I stared at the men and they stared back at us.

One of the men took off his hard hat and scratched his head.

Another man yawned.

Finally Chainsaw Man gave a big sigh. He reached into his jacket pocket and pulled out a phone. He dialled a number, and then spoke.

'Hi, Jason, it's me, Chris. We've run into a bit of a problem, I'm afraid. There's these two crazy girls here, and they seem to be having some kind of love affair with your tree. They ......'

Then he walked away and I couldn't hear any more of the conversation.

A few minutes later he was back. He spoke

to the two men, without even looking at Kate and me.

'Seems like there's a change of plan,' he said. 'We're to go on to do that job in Newtown. It's going to take the rest of the day, so we'd better get a move on.'

Then, without another word, he packed the chainsaw into the jeep, the three men climbed aboard, and seconds later they were gone.

The field seemed strangely silent, with just Kate and me left behind.

'You're so brave, Eva,' she said in the end. 'You were clinging on to Jeremy like nothing would ever make you let go.'

I laughed. 'That was just to keep my hands from shaking. I was really scared.'

It was the truth. Now that the men were gone, the seriousness of what I'd just done was beginning to hit me.

'What are we going to do now?' I asked, as I looked at the tyre-tracks on the grass, and the yellow fence that the men had left behind.

Kate sighed. 'I don't know. But we'll have to think of something. Those men aren't going to give up that easily. They'll be back.'

'But not today,' I said. 'Didn't you hear them? They're going to spend the rest of the day in Newtown. That means we've got at least until tomorrow to come up with a plan.'

Kate nodded slowly. Then she turned around and patted the tree. 'Don't you worry, Jeremy,' she said. 'Eva and I will take good care of you. We won't let them hurt even the smallest of your branches – we promise.'

For a second I agreed with her, and I almost reached out and patted Jeremy too.

Then I remembered that Kate was talking to a tree, and making promises to it.

I sooo didn't want to be part of this.

It was just too weird.

And if Victoria and Ella ever got to hear about it, I would never, ever be allowed to forget it.

Chapter Sixteen

I was up and dressed early the next morning. There was no sign of Kate, and I still didn't dare to call for her. So, feeling slightly nervous, I set off for the Island of Dreams.

When I got to the field, Kate was already there, sitting on an old, faded rug. She looked tired.

'How long have you been here?' I asked.

Kate shrugged.

'Dunno, but it was early when I got here. It was still sort of dark.'

'Sort of dark?'

She gave a tired smile.

'OK, so it was completely dark. I think it was

about five o'clock.'

'Didn't Martha mind you going out so early?'

Kate shook her head.

'Nah, Martha trusts me not to get into trouble. And I couldn't take any chances. I know those men are going to come back. So I had to be here. I had to be ready for them.'

'And when they come back, what are you going to do?'

She shrugged.

'Any bright ideas?'

I wasn't sure how to tell her the good news that I didn't have a single idea, bright or otherwise. But before I could say anything at all, I heard the sound of an engine coming up the hill.

It was the jeep from the day before, with just Chainsaw Man inside. He climbed out and came over to us. Kate jumped up and threw herself against Jeremy.

'Don't you dare touch him,' she hissed.

'So you're still at this nonsense,' he said. 'Well,

have fun, because we just have to finish up another job. We'll be back here by four o'clock this afternoon, and we're not going to have any messing around. We're cutting this tree down whether you like it or not.'

'But why?' I asked. 'Why are you cutting down this perfectly good, perfectly beautiful tree?'

'Because a man from Dublin has bought this field. He wants to build a holiday home here, but your tree, Jasper, or whatever you call him, is in the way.'

'It's Jeremy,' said Kate.

The man rolled his eyes.

'If you say so,' he said.

'But it's a huge field,' I protested. 'The man could build his house anywhere else, and the tree could stay. Why does he have to build on this exact spot?'

The man shrugged.

'I don't know, do I? I don't ask questions. I

just do my job.'

'Well it's a *horrible* job,' said Kate sulkily.

The man laughed, but not in a mean way.

'Look girls,' he said. 'I'm sorry you're upset, but do yourselves a big favour and don't be here when I get back. OK?'

Neither of us answered, so he gave a big sigh, climbed back into his jeep, and drove off with a loud rev of his engine.

'Now what?' asked Kate.

If Kate wanted to know about cool dance moves, or where to buy totally great jeans, and stuff like that, I was her girl.

When had I become the expert on saving trees from being cut down?

But then I looked more closely at Kate. Her face was pale, and her eyes were rimmed with red. She looked like her whole world, and not just a tree, was about to come tumbling down.

And she had no one else to call on. She had no friends, and her only family was an old granny who never seemed to venture outside her own front door.

So, even though I totally didn't want to be involved, I knew it was already much, much too late for that.

'Don't worry, Kate,' I said. 'Leave it to me. I'll think of something.'

⚝   ♥   ♡

I sat on the rug and thought for ages.

'You should be good at this sort of thing,' said Kate after a while. 'Didn't you say that you helped heaps of people before, when you were trying to do what Madame Margarita said?'

'That was sooo different,' I said.

'How?'

'I don't know how. It just was. Now be quiet for a minute and let me think.'

Kate sat quietly and watched me. Her calm expression made me nervous. I could see that she trusted me completely, even though I had no idea of what to do next.

'The man's coming back at four o'clock,' I said after a while.

Kate made a face.

'We know that, but how does it help us?'

'Because we know that's how long we've got to rustle up some support. Those men won't listen to you and me, but if there are more people here, they can't ignore that.'

Kate smiled, but a second later her smile faded away.

'Who's going to come here to support us?'

'Maybe some kids from your school?'

She shook her head violently.

'I'm not popular like you, Eva. Some of the kids in my school call me names and the rest ignore me. None of them would help me.'

I'd been afraid of that. I should have felt really angry on Kate's behalf, but there was no time for that. I had to come up with a tree-saving plan.

'Er ... maybe my mum and dad would come,'
I said 'And Joey. And you could go and get
Martha.'

Kate shook her head again.

'Martha wouldn't come.'

'Er ... maybe Cathy and Lily?'

Now Kate laughed, a loud, scornful laugh.

'No chance. They'd be afraid of damaging
their nails, or messing up their hair.'

She was right, and I felt bad when I realised
that up to recently, I'd have been the same.

Kate folded her arms.

'I'll stay here and keep watch, in case the
men come back early. You go and round up the
crowd.'

I sighed.

Why did I have to get the hard job?

✤　❤　♡

I raced back home, and went into the kitchen
where Mum, Dad and Joey were still eating

their breakfast.

I told them my story.

'Coooool,' said Joey.

'Poor Kate,' said Mum. 'We can't let this happen.'

'I always wanted to be an eco-warrior,' said Dad. 'Will I have time to grow a beard?'

'Seriously,' I said. 'Who's going to come and help us?'

'Me,' shouted Joey. 'And I'll bring all my friends.'

'You've got friends?' I asked in amazement.

Joey ignored my insult.

'Yes, I've got heaps. Well three or four anyway. We play soccer on the beach every day. There's Danny and Simon, and a big guy with red hair – I don't know his name but I'm too afraid to ask him, and there's—'

'OK, enough, already,' I said. 'I don't need to know what they're called.'

Joey shrugged.

'OK. I'll just go and ask them to come and help us save the tree.'

I smiled at him. Who ever would have thought he'd be good for anything?

'I'll come too,' said Mum. 'That poor girl's been through enough already. Just let me do the washing up first.'

Dad laughed.

'You'll save the world, but only once the kitchen's clean?'

Mum pretended to punch him.

'Help me, so,' she said. 'And then we can get on to the important stuff.'

'What about you, Dad?' I asked. 'Will you come and protest?'

'It's not exactly my idea of a fun day out,' he said. 'And I had planned to fix those loose windows at the back of the house, but your mum's right. We can't let this happen. So you go back up there and stay with Kate, and we'll be along in a while.'

On the way back to the field, I met an old man called Miley, who hangs around near the beach, collecting firewood. I told him the story, and he stood there nodding slowly. I wasn't sure if he'd understood.

'It's for Kate,' I said. 'We're doing this for Kate.' Miley smiled.

'Kate's a good girl,' he said.

'So will you come to the big field at three-thirty?' I asked.

He just kept nodding his head ever so slowly. I gave up, and continued up the hill.

'Where's everyone?' asked Kate when I got back. 'I thought you were going to bring a crowd of helpers.'

'Don't worry,' I said, trying to sound confident. 'They'll be here. Now just relax for a while. It's going to be a busy afternoon.'

Chapter Seventeen

Just after half past three, Joey arrived with a trail of four little boys behind him. I could have hugged him, but resisted. Kate couldn't resist though, and Joey pulled away whining, 'If you're going to do that soppy kind of stuff, me and the lads are off.'

I giggled. Kate always seemed so distant, and non-huggable, and I was happy to see a different side to her.

'Don't worry, Joey,' I said. 'Kate just got carried away. It won't happen again.'

Joey looked around. 'So where are the mad men with chainsaws?'

'They're not here yet,' I said. 'But we know

they're coming back, so don't go away.'

'OK,' said Joey. 'Will we climb up the tree to wait for them?'

'And when the men come back we could throw water bombs down on top of them,' said another boy.

'Or rocks,' said a red-haired boy.

I had a horrible feeling he wasn't joking.

'Great idea,' I said. 'That way we'll save the tree, but we'll never get to see it because we'll all be in jail.'

The poor boy was so embarrassed that his hair and face became almost the same colour.

I felt sorry for him. 'I appreciate your enthusiasm,' I said. 'But hopefully we can solve this without any violence.'

Joey stepped forward. 'Me and the lads will play soccer over here,' he said. 'Just call us when you need us.'

As Joey and his friends walked away, Miley appeared. He was carrying a large, dangerous-looking stick.

'Where do you want me?' he asked, waving the stick in the air.

I didn't know whether to laugh or cry.

'Just stand over there,' I said in the end. 'And when we tell you to....well when we think of something to tell you to do, do it, OK?'

Miley nodded and went and sat on the grass near the hedge.

A few minutes later, Mum and Dad arrived. With them were two tall, thin men in hiking gear.

'This is Hans and Friedrich,' said Mum. 'They're tourists from Germany.'

'From Essen,' said one.

'An industrial city in north part of Germany,' said the other.

I looked at Mum trying to ask a question with my eyes.

Where on earth did you find these two?

Mum seemed to understand.

'Your dad and I met Hans and Friedrich on the road up here,' she said. 'We told them what's going on, and they said they'd come with us.'

'We are loving the environment,' said one of them. 'We are wanting that the trees they are not being cutted down.'

'We are wanting that too,' I said giggling, but I stopped when I saw that Kate was glaring at me. She was probably right – this was no laughing matter.

Just then there was the sound of a jeep coming along the road. Everyone stopped talking and turned to look at me.

It seemed like I was in charge.

But what on earth was I supposed to do next?

Long seconds passed, and still everyone was staring at me.

'Er……everyone to their places,' I said desperately, trying to sound like I had a plan.

Most people ignored me. Hans stepped forward and spoke politely.

'Where are our places, please?' he asked.

How on earth was I supposed to know?

Suddenly I remembered a TV programme where a group of people were trying to stop developers from knocking down a community centre.

'Er….how about we make a big circle holding hands around the tree?' I suggested.

People seemed glad to be doing something, and all the adults shuffled into place, with their backs to the tree. I noticed Mum moving quickly so that she wouldn't have to hold Miley's filthy hand. (I didn't really blame her, but how did she expect to save the world if she only wanted to hold clean hands?)

Joey and his friends were still playing soccer and ignored my calls. Kate put her fingers in her mouth and whistled loudly right next to my ear. The boys came running but I wondered if the damage to my hearing was worth it.

By the time the jeep had stopped at the edge

of the field, everyone was in position.

The battle was on.

And it looked like I was the commander-in-chief.

So why did I feel so scared?

The men climbed out of the jeep and walked slowly towards us. They must have been surprised to see a crowd of people standing holding hands around a tree, like we were doing some crazy kind of dance.

Miley let go of Dad's hand, and waved his stick in the air.

'One more step, and I'll brain the lot of you,' he said.

Great.

Looked like I'd invited the local psychopath to join our peaceful protest.

The men stopped walking. Chainsaw Man stepped towards Mum.

'You look like a reasonable woman,' he said.

(Hah. Clearly he's never seen her when I leave

my clothes on the floor of my bedroom.)

Mum smiled, like being a reasonable woman was what she'd always dreamed of becoming.

The man continued, 'Can't you talk some sense into these people? The tree has to go, and delaying it isn't going to help anyone.'

Mum smiled again. 'I understand your position, really I do,' she said. 'The thing is, I agree with everyone else here. This is the only proper tree for miles around, and I don't think it should be cut down. So, basically ... We're. Not. Moving.'

The man stepped backwards.

'OK,' he said. 'Looks like the gloves are off. I'm phoning the police.'

As he spoke, he pulled his mobile phone from his pocket. Before he could dial the number, Joey ran over and tapped him on the arm.

'Hey, Mister,' he said. 'Have you got free calls on that phone?'

'What's that got to do with anything?' asked the man.

'Just, if you haven't, you'll be wasting your money, because there's a big soccer match on in the next village, and all the policemen have gone there. So no one's going to be available to come here.'

'Unless there's a murder,' continued Miley, who looked like he'd be happy to arrange that, no problem.

Chainsaw Man put his phone back into his pocket and scratched his head.

I grabbed Joey as he ran back to his friends.

'Well done, kid,' I said. 'How did you know about the match?'

He grinned. 'There isn't one. I just made it up so he wouldn't phone the police.'

Once again I had to resist the urge to hug him

When had this boy become so clever and useful?

Maybe miracles were possible after all.

Chapter Eighteen

An hour later, not much had changed.

Chainsaw Man had made a few phone calls, and now he and his buddies were sitting in their jeep, staring into the field at the rest of us.

Joey and his friends were playing soccer.

A farmer had parked his tractor in the lane and had come in to see what was going on. Mum was chatting to him about chickens.

'That's really interesting,' I heard her say. 'I think I might start to keep chickens in the autumn.'

I giggled. Not long ago, Mum thought of chickens as things that caterers delivered when she was having a fancy dinner party.

How did she get to the stage where she was thinking of them as things she'd like to have running around her back garden?

Hans and Friedrich were speaking to each other in German. They were probably wondering how their holiday had turned into some crazy escapade with a bunch of mad Irish people.

Miley was sitting propped up against Jeremy. His eyes were closed and he was snoring loudly.

Kate and I were sitting on the rug. I was starting to feel a bit stupid. We were all hanging around ready for a fight, and yet nothing was happening.

We all jumped at the sudden sound of an engine. It was the jeep starting up, and seconds later it had vanished down the road with the three men inside it.

Joey raced over.

'Result,' he cried. 'They're gone. We've won.'

Mum smiled at him.

'I don't think it's that simple, Joey,' she said.

'They've gone for now. But no doubt they'll be back.'

'Not today,' said Dad. 'It's past their finishing up time. I don't think anything else is going to happen here today. And besides......there's this match I want to see, and I know they're showing it on TV in the pub in the village.'

'Yes, sorry, girls,' said Mum. 'I really need to go home and get the tea started.'

The boys all had to go home too, and Hans and Friedrich realised it was time for them to check in to their Bed and Breakfast.

The commotion of everyone leaving woke Miley. He jumped up, grabbed his stick and raced down the hill after everyone else.

The field seemed suddenly quiet with just Kate and me left.

We sat on the rug, and Kate looked at me, 'I suppose you're going away too?' she said.

I shook my head, 'Not yet. I'll stay until I have to go home for dinner. What about you?'

'I'm staying here,' she said.

'I know. But until when?'

She shrugged. 'I don't know. We can't leave Jeremy unguarded. So I'll stay until the danger is over. For a few days anyway.'

'But you can't! Where will you sleep?'

She gave a bigger shrug. 'I can sleep here. I've often done that before.'

'But that was … before … you know … you weren't on your own then.'

'I know,' she said fiercely. 'I was with my dad. But Dad's not here now is he?'

I gulped. Kate hardly ever mentioned her dad, and when she did, it always made me feel embarrassed.

'So I'll have to manage on my own,' she said, in a quieter voice.

'But you said you had a tent then. You—'

Suddenly she grabbed my arm. 'The tent – I forgot I still have it at home. If I get the tent everything will be perfect.'

She stopped talking and put her head down. 'But I can't go and get the tent. I can't leave Jeremy on his own. He needs me.'

'I'll stay here,' I said. 'I'll take good care of Jeremy while you're gone.'

Kate shook her head.

'Thanks, but I can't leave. If I leave, it would be like abandoning him. You'll have to go and get the tent.'

Great. Once again I was getting the tough job.

As I stood up to go, Kate seemed a bit uneasy.

'You don't need to chat to Martha or anything,' she said. 'Just get the tent, and come straight back, OK?'

That sounded like a good plan to me, so I nodded, and set off down the field.

✩ ♥ ♡

The house looked even creepier than before. I felt like a small, lost child in a fairy story, as I took a deep breath and knocked on the door. I jumped as the door creaked open at my touch. I jumped even higher when an old woman stuck her head out through the open window next to me. She had a thin, wrinkled face and long, white, straggly hair. She was wearing a shirt that looked like it was about a hundred years old.

'Who are you and what do you want?' she barked in a deep voice.

'Er … I'm Eva. I'm Kate's friend.'

She gave a witch-like laugh.

'Are you indeed? Now why are you here? I hope Kate's not in some kind of trouble.'

I thought about telling her the truth, but I wasn't brave enough.

'No,' I said slowly. 'She's not in trouble.'

Martha leaned farther out the window.

'What's Kate been telling you anyway?'

I took a step backwards.

'Nothing. She just told me about her dad, that's all.'

Martha narrowed her eyes. 'That wasn't my fault, you know. I hope she told you that.'

I took another step backwards. This was totally weird. How could Kate's dad being knocked down have been Martha's fault?

Surely she hadn't been driving the truck?

How awful would that have been?

I decided it was time to get down to business.

'Kate and I are going camping,' I said. 'So I need to get her tent. She said it's in the bottom of the wardrobe in her bedroom.'

'You're not coming in here,' said Martha.

She needn't have worried. There was *no way* I was going into that house without a team of minders to protect me.

'Maybe you'd be kind enough to pass the tent out then please?' I said in my sweetest voice.

Martha didn't reply, but she vanished from the window. Seconds later she was back and she shoved a black canvas bag out the window and onto the ground. I picked up the bag and ran

towards the gate. I could hear the sound of the
window slamming behind me.

Chapter Nineteen

It took me ages to get back to the field. When I got there, Kate was sitting cross-legged on the faded old rug, like some kind of ancient hippy.

I dropped the tent to the ground and threw myself on to the rug.

'That must be the heaviest tent in the world,' I said. 'My arms are killing me.'

'What did Martha say?' asked Kate.

'Not much,' I said.

Kate looked relieved when I said that, and I wondered why. What dark secret about her grandmother was she trying to keep from me?

'Thanks for getting the tent, Eva,' she said then.

'You're welcome,' I said, and then we sat in silence for a long time.

'Will I help you to put the tent up?' I asked after a while.

Kate jumped to her feet.

'Thanks, Eva. I don't really know how to do it. That was always Dad's job. He used to put up the tent, and I'd search for flowers to decorate it, and arrange our beds inside it and everything.'

I had a sudden picture of a much younger Kate, with long hair, and a smiling face, running around the field and playing with her dad.

But that was too sad, so I pushed it out of my mind, and helped Kate to empty everything out of the canvas bag.

It wasn't one of those modern tents that just pop up all on their own. There were ropes and poles and pegs, and none of it seemed to make much sense at first. In the end, after lots of disasters, and lots of very, very rude words from Kate, the tent was up – sort of. It leaned very much one way, and it looked like the first gust of wind would blow it away. Luckily though, it was a still, calm evening, and there was a small chance that the tent might stay upright until the morning.

Kate and I sat on the rug admiring our work. Now that we weren't busy any more, I realised that my stomach was rumbling. I hadn't had anything to eat for ages and ages. But how could I go home and eat my dinner knowing that Kate was up here, alone and hungry?

Just then I heard the unmistakable sound of Joey's poor attempt at whistling.

Seconds later I could smell the unmistakable smell of meat and onions.

Seconds later again, Joey was ducking away from one of Kate's hugs.

As soon as he felt safe, Joey put a huge basket down on the grass next to the tent.

'Paula sent food for both of you,' he said. 'And Eva, she says you're to be home by nine-thirty.'

Then he skipped away, still whistling tunelessly.

Kate and I didn't speak for ten minutes as we devoured the huge bowls of Mum's special spaghetti bolognaise. Then we packed the empty bowls and cutlery back into the basket. After that we lay on the rug and looked up at the sky.

'Your mum's great at cooking,' said Kate.

I was feeling guilty again when she continued, 'Martha says my mum was a disaster in the kitchen. She couldn't boil an egg without burning it.'

'Even so, you must wish she was still here,' I said, feeling suddenly brave.

Kate shook her head.

'It's hard to miss what you never knew you had.'

I didn't agree, but didn't feel like arguing, so instead I changed the subject.

'I'd love to spend the night here with you,' I said, 'but I know there's no point in even asking

Mum and Dad. I know they won't let me.'

'It's OK,' said Kate. 'I don't mind.'

'But what if Chainsaw Man comes back?'

She sighed.

'I don't know what I'll do if that happens, but I'll think of something.'

'But won't you be afraid up here all on your own?'

'No. I've got Jeremy to take care of me.'

I turned to look at her to see if she was joking, but it didn't look like she was. Her face was perfectly serious. It seemed like she really did feel safe in this place, near this tree.

And that meant I had to make sure nothing changed – ever.

A while later, I checked my phone.

'Oh no, it's half nine!' I cried, as I grabbed the basket and jumped to my feet. 'I'm late. I have to get back or Mum and Dad will go crazy. Are you sure you're going to be OK?'

Kate stood up too. 'It's nice of you to worry

about me, but I'll be OK.'

And then for the first time ever, she hugged me. I hugged her back, and then set off down the hill.

Near the end, I turned and waved. 'I'll be back first thing in the morning,' I called.

Kate waved back. 'I'll be here.'

And then I went home.

Chapter Twenty

When I went to bed that night, I couldn't sleep. I tried to think of fun stuff, like hanging out with Ella and Victoria and Ruby, but nothing worked. The same picture kept pushing itself into my brain – a picture of Kate, all alone in the small, dark tent.

Life just wasn't fair.

It wasn't fair that Kate had no mum or dad.

It wasn't fair that she'd ended up living with that cross Martha in that horrible falling-down house.

And it wasn't fair that the one place in the whole world that was special to her was about to be destroyed.

I couldn't do anything to change the first two things, but I sure could do something about the third.

Suddenly it became the most important thing in my life.

Even if I had to chain myself to the tree for six months, I'd make sure that it wasn't cut down.

✫ ♥ ♡

Another long hour passed, and still I couldn't sleep. This was crazy. I climbed out of bed and got dressed, pulling on my warmest fleece and tracksuit bottoms. Then I tip-toed downstairs, carefully avoiding the creaky step that Dad hadn't got around to fixing yet.

I found a scrap of paper and wrote a note – *Mum and Dad, decided to get up early and go to the tree with Kate. See you later. Eva. xxx*

Hoping they wouldn't guess exactly how early I'd got up, I slipped through the back door, closing it softly behind me.

It was a clear night, and the light of the moon made everything a creepy silvery-grey colour.

I didn't want to frighten Kate, so I called softly as I got close to the tent. I could hear her fumbling with the tent-flaps, and seconds later she was kneeling at the tent opening, grinning happily.

'You came,' she said.

'You don't look surprised.'

Kate shook her head.

'I'm not surprised. You're my friend. I knew you'd come.'

I didn't know how to answer that, so I just crawled into the tent and lay down. Kate edged back in beside me.

'Now you're here, I'm not afraid any more,' she said. 'So I can leave the tent-flaps open.'

'But I thought you weren't afraid anyway. I thought Jeremy was minding you.'

She giggled.

'He was doing his best, but it's nice to have a human being here too. Just in case.'

Neither of us spoke for a while. The air was warm, and there was a smell of damp canvas that was kind of nice.

I was just dropping off to sleep, when Kate spoke.

'I can see Lyra,' she said.

I sat up quickly.

'Who's Lyra? What's she doing here? Is she on our side?'

'Lyra's not a person. It's a constellation.'

I lay down again, relieved.

'Look,' said Kate pointing through the open tent-flap. 'See that bright star over there?'

I shook my head. 'What bright star? They all look the same to me.'

Kate patiently explained, and after a while I could see what she was talking about. When I looked closely, I could see differences between the stars. Some were brighter than others, some twinkled more, and some were almost invisible – just the faintest points of light. Then she showed me how some of the stars were arranged in shapes. She was really patient, and explained everything carefully. It was totally cool, and I forgot how tired I had been a few minutes earlier. By the time I fell asleep, I'd had my first, very thorough, lesson in astronomy.

☆ ♥ ♡

When I woke up, a greyish light filled the tent. It was chilly, and I pulled the old rug over me to try to get warm. Kate was still asleep. She looked young and peaceful. Her short hair was all spiky-looking.

She looked like she needed someone to take care of her.

I wished she had someone to take care of her.

Just then I heard the sound of heavy boots coming along the road. I grabbed Kate and shook her.

'Wake up. Someone's coming.'

Kate jumped up and together we scrambled out of the tent. Just above the hedge, I could see the bobble of a hat bouncing along in time with the footsteps. It would have been funny, if I hadn't been so scared.

Kate gave a big sigh. 'You don't have to worry, Eva. I know that hat. It's just Martha.'

I stepped back towards the tent, as if the flimsy canvas could protect me from the cranky old woman.

Soon Martha was beside us. She looked totally bizarre in a faded old skirt, a huge rugby jersey, big heavy mens' boots and a purple woolly hat. She was carrying a basket.

'I've brought you some food and a hot drink,' she said.

For one second I thought she was like the evil queen in Snow White.

Had she come to poison us?

Did I dare to touch anything that came out of that basket?

I waited for Kate to answer.

'Thanks, Martha,' she said.

Martha gave a small smile. Then she put the basket on the ground and walked away.

When she was gone, Kate reached in to the basket and took out a flask and two cups. She opened the flask.

'Mmmmmmm,' she said. 'Hot chocolate. Martha makes the yummiest hot chocolate.'

I pulled out a bundle wrapped in a tea-cloth. Inside were four warm scones, with melting butter dripping down the sides.

All thoughts of poison vanished from my mind as we drank the hot chocolate and ate the scones in seconds.

'That was really nice of Martha,' I said, when I finally stopped for breath.

'You sound surprised.'

That's because I thought she was a total witch.

I hesitated.

'Well ... I am a bit surprised. I thought Martha was ... well you know ... kind of mean.'

Kate laughed.

'She's not mean. She just gets very grumpy sometimes – when her bones hurt. When she's like that, I usually just keep out of her way.'

'I think maybe her bones were hurting her yesterday when I went to get the tent,' I said, and Kate gave a small giggle, before turning serious again.

'Martha's had a hard life,' she said. 'Her husband, that's my grandad, died when she was very young, and my dad was her only child. She still feels guilty about what happened to him.'

Suddenly that reminded me of something.

'Yesterday, Martha said it wasn't her fault, you know ... about your dad. She wasn't driving the truck, was she?'

Kate looked at me like I was crazy.

'Of course not,' she said.

'So why does she feel guilty?'

Kate put her head down.

'Weeeeell, it's complicated. I suppose Martha thinks that somehow she could have saved Dad.'

That sounded a bit crazy to me.

Martha wasn't even there.

And if she had been there, what could she have done? How can you save anyone if they step out in front of a big truck?

Did Martha think it was her fault because she hadn't taught her son the Safe Cross Code properly when he was small?

Anyway, I *so* didn't like talking about Kate's dead father, so I changed the subject.

'I think I'd better go home and tell Mum and Dad I'm not dead or kidnapped or something,' I said. 'Will you be OK here for a bit?'

Kate nodded.

'Sure. Me and Jeremy – we'll be just fine.'

Chapter Twenty-One

I didn't really tell a lie when I got back to the house. I just didn't exactly tell the truth.

'Hi Mum, hi Dad,' I called as I let myself in the back door.

'Hi darling,' said Dad. 'It's not like you to be up before us. What time did you get up?'

I tried to look innocent. 'Er … I'm not really sure. I didn't check my phone. It was early though.'

(Like the middle of the night!)

Mum rubbed my head like I was a puppy.

'You're being really nice to Kate. We're proud of you.'

This was getting embarrassing, so I put a

quick stop to it.

'I just came back to say "hi",' I said. 'So, hi. Now I think I'll go back and keep Kate company for a while.'

I ran out again, before anyone could argue, and minutes later I was back in the field with Kate.

I sat down beside her.

'Now what?' I asked.

'Now we just wait to see what's going to happen. Or did you have other plans?'

I couldn't answer her. I hadn't known what to expect when Mum and Dad dragged me on this holiday, but I *so* hadn't expected this.

I lay back on the rug and looked up at the sky.

'Pity the stars are gone,' I said.

Kate giggled.

'They're not gone. They're up there in the daytime too. You just can't see them, that's all.'

It was a strange thought. I wondered if that was the way Kate felt about her dad? Was he still somewhere, watching over her, like the invisible stars? I was deciding if I dared to say this to Kate, when my thoughts were interrupted by the sound of feet marching along the road.

I sat up in time to see Joey marching into the field, followed by nine or ten little boys. They started to chant, 'Listen to us – we're making a fuss. Listen to me – save the tree.'

Kate stood up, and laughed as the boys marched closer.

They marched right up to the edge of the rug, and then they stayed there, marching on the spot, chanting their refrain over and over, and ignoring Kate's giggles.

In the end, Joey raised one hand in the air.

'Troops, at ease,' he said, and instantly the boys stopped marching and stood quietly.

'Where do you want us?' asked Joey.

'Er……,' I began, not really sure what to do with this band of determined little boys. 'Why don't you go over there and play soccer for a while, like yesterday.' I said. 'And we'll call you if we need you.'

'Yay, soccer,' screeched one of the boys pulling a soccer ball from underneath his sweat-shirt. Then they all ran off to the other side of the field.

Half an hour later, the boys were still kicking their football. Kate and I had plenty to occupy us though, as it was getting very crowded in the shade of the tree.

Hans and Friedrich were back, accompanied by three Japanese tourists.

'We meet them in the Bed and Breakfast,' said Hans.

'And they want to help saving the tree,' said Friedrich.

The Japanese tourists kept smiling and nodding and taking endless photographs. I wondered what their friends back home would make of the bizarre scene.

Mum and Dad were there, with a small, quiet

man who ran the local shop. The woman from the pub was there too, chatting to some of the local farmers. Miley was there, with a huge round red-faced woman that Kate said was his wife. She kept shaking our hands and thanking us and saying that it was nice to get out for a change – something that made me think that she must have a very, very sad life.

People sat around on rugs and deck-chairs, and chatted like this was some kind of holiday camp.

But the biggest surprise of all was when Martha appeared, carrying a small three-legged stool. She put the stool on the grass and sat down heavily.

'What are you doing here?' asked Kate, (a bit rudely, I thought).

Martha didn't seem to mind though.

'Well, Girleen,' she said. 'If family don't stick together we're all lost, aren't we?'

And no one could think of anything to say to that.

A few minutes later, Kate grabbed my arm.

'Look over there,' she hissed.

I turned to where she was pointing and gasped.

'It's Lily,' I said.

Kate giggled.

'It can't be. In the summer, there's no such person as Lily. There's only CathyandLily. They don't exist on their own.'

She couldn't say any more, as Lily was right next to us. As usual she looked totally fabulous. Her hair was all smooth and silky, and she was wearing a cool dress and sparkly flip-flops.

I wished I hadn't spent most of the night in a field.

I wished I didn't look exactly like someone who had spent most of the night in a field. My hair was all messy, and I knew that my tracksuit bottoms were filthy. I didn't have to look at Kate to know that she was her usual untidy self.

Had Lily come to mock us?

Was she taking everything in, so she could go back and tell Cathy all about it?

Then I noticed that Lily looked kind of embarrassed.

'Er … I heard what you're doing,' she said. 'And I think it's great. Can I join in?'

Kate and I didn't answer. I still thought it was some kind of a sick joke. Was Cathy going to appear from behind a ditch, laughing at us all?

Now Lily looked even more embarrassed by our silence.

'That's if … if you don't mind,' she said softly.

Kate and I looked at each other, and I tried to read what was in her eyes, but found that I couldn't.

Suddenly I felt angry. Lily had been mean to Kate for years, so why should we be nice to her now?

'I don't think ….' I began, but I stopped speaking when Kate put a firm hand on my arm.

'Of course we don't mind,' she said. 'There's

plenty of room for one more. Thanks for coming.'

I gazed at Kate.

How could she be so generous and forgiving?

Kate and I scrunched over to the side of the rug, (which I wished wasn't so old and faded), and Lily sat down beside us.

Even though there were so many people around, and there was lots of activity, I couldn't think of anything to say.

Kate wasn't much better. She just sat there, looking out towards the sea, like the girl who'd always been so mean to her wasn't sitting right next to us, breathing our air, and getting the same dirty bottom from the same grubby old rug.

In the end the silence was too much for me. 'So where's Cathy?' I asked.

'She's gone to France,' said Lily. 'To tennis camp. She's not coming back for the rest of the summer.'

Now I felt angry again. So that was why she was here. Her best friend had gone away, so she'd decided she'd have to put up with second best – with Kate and me.

There were so many words racing around my mind that I couldn't get any of them out.

Then Lily spoke again. 'I'm sorry,' she said, looking at Kate. 'I think that maybe Cathy and I have been a bit mean to you.'

A bit mean? How about very, very, very mean?

Kate didn't answer. She just sat there looking at Lily. Lily went red again.

'It's not really my fault ….' she began.

At last I managed to get some words out.

'*Not your fault?*' I said so loudly that everyone in the field turned to stare. Even the Japanese tourists turned to look at me as if I was just about to say something really important. One took out his camera and took a picture of me before I even had time to stick my tongue out at him. I waited until they got tired of staring, and continued talking to Lily in a lower voice.

'How could it not be your fault? You said all those awful things. I heard you myself. And I didn't see anyone holding a gun to your head.'

'What awful things?' asked Kate, suddenly reminding me that I hadn't told her about them.

'Oh … just general bad stuff,' I said. Then I turned back to Lily. 'Well?'

Lily gave a big sigh. 'When I'm with Cathy, I feel like I have to impress her.'

'That's stupid,' I said.

'I know I should be stronger,' said Lily. 'It's just that Cathy can be very persuasive. She's very strong-willed. She's—'

'She's a bully,' I finished for her.

Lily nodded slowly.

'Yes. I suppose you're right. Cathy's a bully, and I let myself be bullied. And I let her make me into a bully too. She's done it for years, so I stopped noticing that it was happening. I know it's not a good excuse, but it's the only one I can offer you. Anyway … I'm sorry, Kate – for everything.'

We both looked at Kate.

Kate shrugged. 'So you said some bad stuff. That's OK. I'm used to that kind of thing.'

I felt like punching someone or something. I turned to look at Jeremy, but resisted. I knew Kate would *not* be happy if I touched him in anger. So I punched the ground instead. I hit my knuckle on a stone, and it really hurt, but it couldn't distract me from my anger.

How dare everyone be so mean to Kate?

She was kind and gentle and funny and clever, and just because she dressed differently to everyone else, why did that give people a right to be mean to her?

Who had the right to hurt this girl who had never hurt anyone or anything in her entire life?

And then I had a horrible thought. When I first met Kate, I didn't want anything to do with her. I judged her by her looks, and did all

I could to get away from her. I wasn't as mean as Cathy and Lily, but I wasn't exactly an angel either.

I felt really angry, and really sad and really guilty – all at once. I couldn't think of anything to say to make things right, though. So I just put my arm around Kate, and we sat there, waiting for something to happen.

Chapter Twenty-Two

At around one o'clock, there was a flurry of activity when a woman came marching up the lane. She was shouting loudly.

'Billy, if you're up here I'm going to kill you. Don't you know it's time for your lunch?'

I didn't know who Billy was, but it wasn't hard to find out. The red-haired boy, the biggest and toughest-looking of Joey's friends looked like he was going to die of embarrassment. He picked up the soccer ball and started to walk towards the woman.

'But Muuuuuuum,' he wailed. 'I can't go home. I've got to save the tree.'

His mother wasn't impressed.

'You can save all the trees you like,' she shouted. 'But not until you've had your lunch.'

She was a fierce-looking woman, and Billy probably knew there wasn't much point in arguing with her.

He threw the ball towards Joey.

'Mind my ball,' he said, and then he followed his mother out of the field.

The mention of lunch made me feel hungry and I had a fair idea that I wasn't the only one. People were starting to look at their watches, and to shuffle restlessly.

Lily reached into her beautiful designer handbag and pulled out a totally cool phone. 'I'll ring my mum,' she said. 'She'll bring us some food. She runs a catering business.'

Half an hour later, a shiny silver car drew up at the entrance to the field and a smartly-dressed woman climbed out.

'Liliana, come and help me please,' she called.

'Liliana?' I said, trying not to laugh.

Lily made a face at me. 'I was called after my grandmother. Now, can you guys help? Knowing my mum, there'll be a lot to carry.'

'Sure thing, Liliana,' I said, and the three of us laughed as we set off to unload the car.

There was so much stuff, it took us four trips to carry it all from the car to the tree. Lily's mum had thought of everything. She'd brought disposable barbeques, heaps of chicken legs and sausages, big crusty rolls, tubs of salad, paper plates and cups and bottles of lemonade.

Kate tried to hide the paper plates and cups behind the lemonade bottles.

'We can't let Jeremy see these,' she said. 'They might be made from one of his cousins.'

I looked at her impatiently. Everything was going so well – was she going to spoil it all by acting crazy?

Then I saw that she was laughing, so I laughed too, and then Lily joined in, followed by everyone else – even Hans and Friedrich, who kept tapping my dad on the shoulder, saying, 'What is the joke, please?'

Lily's mum set to work, and soon we were all eating happily. When every scrap of food was finished, Martha reached in to the big rucksack she'd brought with her.

'Anyone for a chocolate bun?' she asked, and then she had to back away as everyone rushed at her. She quickly had everyone lining up like they were at school, and she produced a bag of what looked like a hundred buns.

'How did you know to bring so many?' I asked.

Martha laughed. 'I used to be a Girl Guide, back in the last century, so I like to be prepared.'

As we were eating the last of the crumbs from the chocolate buns, Hans went off, and returned a few minutes later, carrying a guitar. He sat on the grass and began to play, with Friedrich singing along. The song was in German, so of course no one else knew the words, but when he got to the chorus, everyone hummed in tune, except for my dad, who managed to be totally out of tune with everyone else.

Hans continued to play, and after a while, the Japanese tourists passed around a big bag of sweets to share, and then we all sat in the sunshine, sucking our sweets and listening to the music and thinking that life was just perfect.

And then the sound of a jeep coming along the lane ruined everything.

Chapter Twenty-Three

He stepped out of the jeep and walked slowly towards us. He wasn't carrying a chainsaw, but he'd always be Chainsaw Man to us.

He walked across the field, and stood staring at us, with his arms folded. One by one, people stopped humming along to the music, and soon Hans stopped strumming his guitar.

Miley's wife had been dozing, but now she looked up and smiled at Chainsaw Man. 'Oh, someone else to join the party,' she said happily. 'I'm afraid you're too late for the barbecue, but there might be a few sweets left or maybe even a nice chocolate bun. Now move along girls, and make room on your rug for the nice man.'

Miley turned to his wife, and explained the situation. She was not happy when she heard the truth. She picked up Miley's stick and shook it at Chainsaw Man.

'Go away, you bad man,' she shouted. 'We're having a lovely party here, and we're not about to let you ruin it.'

I realised that it was only because of Chainsaw Man that we were having the lovely party, but that seemed a bit complicated to explain to Miley's wife.

Chainsaw Man took a few steps backwards, until he was out of range of Miley's stick. Then he said to no one in particular, 'I don't suppose any of you is ready to talk sense?'

In reply, everyone got to their feet, and made a circle around the tree, just like we had done the day before. (Only now, because there were more of us, the circle was bigger and stragglier than ever.)

Chainsaw Man kept trying.

'Anyone got anything sensible to say?'

Joey began to chant, 'Listen to us – we're making a fuss. Listen to me – save the tree.'

By the time he got to the second line, his friends had joined in. They sang it over and over again, and everyone chanted along, except for the Japanese who only managed to say 'tree' at the end of the last line. Hans stepped out of the circle, picked up his guitar, and began to strum along in time to the chant.

Chainsaw Man scratched his head. 'You're all mad,' he said, and then he walked slowly back towards his jeep. The chant continued while Chainsaw Man spoke on his phone. At one stage, he held the phone towards us, as if he wanted the person on the other end to hear us.

Joey saw this and laughed.

'Louder, lads,' he said, and the chant grew louder and faster, until it was just a rush of words, impossible to understand.

Soon Chainsaw Man clicked off his phone and put it into his pocket. He walked back across the field towards us, stopping only when he saw Miley's wife reaching for the stick.

'It's out of my hands now,' he said. 'I've called the police. They're on their way. They'll be here in ten minutes.'

The chanting stopped and there was an uneasy silence.

All kinds of awful pictures raced through my mind.

I could see fleets of armoured vehicles, with bars on the windows.

I could see battalions of helmeted policemen, clutching shields and batons.

I could see the poor Japanese tourists taking home lots of pictures of the inside of an Irish jail.

This so wasn't funny any more.

✮　♥　♡

Minutes later, there was the sound of a car coming along the road. Everyone shuffled closer together.

The car stopped, and there was the slam of a single door. A policeman walked into the field.

'Sure that's only Gerry,' said the shopkeeper.

Beside me, Kate whispered, 'Gerry's the policeman from the next village. Most people here know him well.'

There was a big sigh of relief as all the locals greeted Gerry like he was their oldest friend.

'How's the wife?' asked Miley.

'Any news of my stolen bicycle?' asked one of the farmers.

'Are you free for a game of cards later?' asked the man from the shop.

The poor policeman looked embarrassed.

'Hello, everyone,' he said gruffly. 'I hear there's been a bit of trouble.'

'So do something about it,' prompted Chainsaw Man.

'Like what?'

'You could arrest these people.'

The policeman looked from the big crowd of people to the small car that was parked next to the field.

'All of them?'

'Maybe just the ringleaders,' said Chainsaw Man, staring at Kate and me.

'I'd have to call for reinforcements,' said the policeman. 'And that could take hours – or days.'

Chainsaw Man groaned.

'Any other bright ideas?' he said.

The policeman nodded.

'You could come to the station with me and file a report. Or you could apply for an injunction to make these people go away.'

'What's an injunction?' I asked Mum.

'It's a legal procedure and sometimes it takes months and months,' she said, smiling.

Just then Chainsaw Man's phone rang.

He pulled it out of his pocket and had a short conversation. Then he switched it off.

'Good news,' he said.

'What good news, you evil man?' said Miley's wife.

Chainsaw Man actually smiled.

'The good news is I'm getting a half-day. The owner of the field, Mr Phillips, is coming down tomorrow, and he can deal with the lot of you.'

Joey and his friends began to cheer.

'Yay, we won! We won!' they shouted.

I wasn't so sure.

Was that good news?

Had we won?

Could it possibly have been that easy?

Chainsaw Man probably didn't care much what happened as long as he got paid. I had a funny feeling that the owner of the field wouldn't be quite so easy to get rid of.

Chainsaw Man was still standing there.

'You can all go home now,' he said. 'Nothing's

going to happen here until tomorrow. Mr Phillips won't be here until eleven at the earliest.'

Nobody moved.

'You're wasting your time,' said Chainsaw Man. 'Nothing's going to happen. Trust me.'

Miley's wife waved her stick.

'Why should we trust you?'

Chainsaw Man took a step backwards.

'Because while you're around, I couldn't tell a lie – I wouldn't dare.'

Everyone laughed, and then Chainsaw Man walked back to his jeep and drove off.

The policeman addressed the crowd.

'I know you don't mean any harm, but maybe it would be best for everyone if you just forgot about this whole thing, and let the men get on with what they're paid to do.'

No one answered, and the policeman walked slowly away.

'Tell Mary to drop over later to pick up that nice leg of lamb I've been saving for her,' called one of the farmers after him, and everyone laughed.

'Now what?' said Dad as soon as the policeman had driven away.

'You can all do what you want,' said Kate. 'I'm staying here. I'm not taking any chances.'

Martha came over and patted her shoulder.

'That's my girl,' she said, and I laughed as Kate gave an embarrassed smile.

Mum came over and hugged me.

'I'm proud of you too, Eva,' she said, giving Kate a chance to laugh at me. 'But I have to go home and get the dinner started. If you want to stay here for a while, I'll send Joey up with something for you to eat – and something for your friends too.'

I looked at Kate and Lily.

Were they both my friends now?

Did that mean they were friends with each other?

Was this the weirdest thing ever?

Chapter Twenty-Four

Soon most people did wander away, probably remembering that they had lives that didn't involve sitting around fields trying to stop trees from being chopped down.

In the end only Kate, Lily and I remained.

Kate stood up and started to pick up the fencing tape that had been trampled into the grass around the tree.

'Jeremy gets upset when there's a mess around him,' she said.

I hate it when she says weird stuff like that.

I looked to see what Lily thought. She was laughing.

'You say the craziest stuff, Kate,' she said, but

in a nice way. Then she went on. 'I remember your dad once—'

I was just wondering how come Lily was brave enough to mention Kate's dad, when Kate raced over and stood right in front of Lily.

'Don't talk about my dad,' she said fiercely.

'But—' began Lily.

'Don't even mention him,' said Kate. 'If you say one more thing about him I'll—'

Lily raised her hands as if to surrender.

'Don't worry,' she said. 'I won't mention him again. I promise.'

She looked at me, and I shrugged. How was I supposed to know why Kate was being so defensive? Most of the time I could only give the wildest guess as to what was going on in her mind.

Kate sat down again, and after a minute, she spoke quietly.

'Sorry for shouting at you, Lily. All that family stuff is private, and I don't like talking about it.'

Lily smiled. 'That's OK,' she said.

Then she stared at Kate for so long that it was beginning to be a bit rude.

'Know what, Kate?' she said in the end.

I sat up straight, afraid that there was going to be a big row.

'What?' asked Kate.

'You should wear a hairband,' said Lily. 'It would really suit you.'

I breathed a big sigh of relief.

Kate looked at her blankly, but Lily didn't seem to notice. She was busy scrabbling around in her hand-bag.

'I think I might have one in here,' she said. 'And short hair held back with a hairband is the latest thing.'

She pulled out a cool green hairband and a cute little pink hairbrush decorated with small red hearts.

'May I?' she said, and without waiting for an answer, she started to brush Kate's hair.

I expected Kate to shout at her, but she didn't. She just sat there meekly while Lily worked.

By the time Lily had finished with Kate's hair, it looked completely different – all shiny and nice. Then Lily put the hairband on Kate, using it to hold back part of her fringe.

'Wow,' I said.

Kate looked completely different. She gave a big smile and I gasped.

How come I'd never noticed how pretty she was?

Lily found a small mirror in her bag and held it up so Kate could see herself. Kate looked in the mirror for a long time. Then her cheeks began to go pink, and a slow smile spread over her face.

'Thanks, Lily,' she said.

Lily rooted in her bag again. 'Maybe it's time for a bit of lip-gloss,' she suggested.

Kate looked interested, but when Lily produced the lip-gloss and leaned towards Kate, Kate jumped back like Lily was holding a poisonous snake to her face.

'Don't do it,' she said in a panicky voice. 'I thought it was for you.'

Lily and I laughed, and Lily put the lip-gloss back into her bag.

'I'm not giving up,' she said. 'I bet I'll have you wearing lip-gloss before the week is out.'

'Bet you won't,' said Kate.

I looked at my two new friends, wondering who was going to win that strange bet.

Lily still wasn't finished though.

'Why do you always wear tracksuits?' she asked Kate.

That was something I'd wondered about too, but I'd never dared to ask. Lily seemed to have a way of asking that wasn't insulting though.

Kate thought for a while. Then she shrugged.

'Don't know, really. I just do.'

Lily wagged her finger at her.

'Well you shouldn't. You should wear nice clothes.'

Kate put on a sulky face.

'Martha hasn't got much money, and nice clothes are expensive.'

I turned to look at Lily. How was she going to answer that?

Lily tossed her head.

'That's just stupid,' she said. 'You don't have to be a millionaire to dress nicely.'

'Lily's right,' I said. 'When both my parents lost their jobs last year, I didn't know how I was going to manage without the weekly shopping trips I was used to. But after a while, I got used to just buying the occasional nice thing.'

Kate didn't look convinced, but she smiled anyway.

'I like those jeans you were wearing the other day, Eva,' she said. 'They're not too girly or sparkly. I *hate* sparkly stuff.'

I smiled and tried not to stare at Lily's sparkly flip-flops.

'I got those jeans in a sale,' I said. 'And because

they're kind of plain, they go with everything.'

Kate leaned over and felt the edge of Lily's totally cool cardigan. 'That's lovely,' she said.

Lily smiled. 'Thanks. And it wasn't that expensive. I got it on the internet.'

Kate put her head down. I knew why. She didn't have internet. She didn't even have a computer.

Suddenly Lily realised what she had said.

'Sorry,' she said. 'Anyway, I've got loads of clothes. I can give you something.'

'I don't need charity,' said Kate.

Lily just sighed. 'I don't mean charity. I can lend you something. It's what I do with all my friends.'

I nodded. 'She's right. I do that too, with my friends Victoria and Ella. Even Ruby, who's not that into fashion, has one or two cool things she lends me.'

Kate looked doubtful. 'I'm not used to having friends. How am I meant to know what friends do?'

I hugged her.

'You've got friends now, so just do what we say. OK?'

'Are all friends as bossy as you two?' asked Kate, and we all laughed.

Chapter Twenty-Five

Awhile later, Joey showed up with a big basket of food.

'Paula said you can stay out until ten tonight, Eva,' he said. 'But if you're any later, she's going to come up here and drag you home by the ear.'

'Really?' I said, shocked.

Joey laughed. 'I made up the bit about dragging you home by the ear, but she did say to be home by ten.'

I sighed. I'd thought of begging Mum and Dad to let me stay all night with Kate, but it looked like there was no point. Parents can be an awful pain sometimes.

Joey went off, and Kate, Lily and I dived in to

the food. It's funny how hungry you get when you're trying to save the world.

There was a big lasagne and loads of drippy garlic bread and then yummy lemon cookies. We ate every single scrap and then we lay back on the rug and looked at the darkening sky and talked about nothing.

It was a bit weird. I felt like I was a million miles away from my real life. Victoria's phone was still broken, so I hadn't been in touch with her for ages. She didn't know anything about the tree, or the protest or about my new friends.

Kate was telling us a funny story about Martha trying to catch a crazy chicken when Lily looked at her watch. 'Oh no,' she said. 'It's five to ten. I have to go.'

I jumped up too. 'Me too,' I said.

Kate stayed lying on the rug.

'Why don't you go home?' I said. 'They can't cut the tree down in the dark. And you can come back real early in the morning.'

Kate shook her head. 'No. I'm staying here,' she said. 'It just feels like the right thing to do.'

I hadn't known Kate for very long, but I knew there was no point in arguing with her once her mind was made up.

'I'll get back as soon as I can,' I said.

Then I gave her a quick hug and walked away with Lily.

✧　♥　♡

When I got home, Joey was playing on the old tyre that Dad had hung from a tree, and Mum and Dad were sitting in the garden having a cup of tea. I sat on the grass beside them.

'Tell Eva about the Japanese people,' said Mum.

Dad smiled, 'I had a long chat with them this afternoon.'

'I thought they didn't speak much English,' I said.

Mum laughed, 'They don't. The chat involved

a lot of sign language.'

'Anyway,' said Dad. 'It seems that the Japanese have this special tradition called "hanami". When the cherry blossom is in flower, all the workers have lunch outside under the trees, and have a kind of party to celebrate the flowers.'

'That's so cool,' I said.

'And it explains why those nice Japanese people are so interested in helping you to save the tree,' said Mum.

'Who cares about Japanese people and their cherry blossom,' said Joey, jumping off his swing and running over to us, 'I much prefer Friedrich.'

'Friedrich?' said Dad.

'He's one of the Germans,' I explained. 'The one without the guitar. Why do you like him so much, Joey?'

'Because he's an amazing soccer player,' said Joey. 'He used to play in the German second division.'

'Wow!' said Dad impressed.

'And he's going to give me and the lads a coaching session tomorrow.'

Mum smiled. 'This is turning into an amazing holiday,' she said. 'We're meeting such interesting people.'

'So even if we win the lottery, you don't want to go back to Tuscany?' asked Dad.

Mum shrugged. 'Maybe someday,' she said, looking like she didn't care much either way.

I stood up. 'I can't stay chatting all night,' I said. 'I've got a big day tomorrow, and I need my beauty sleep.'

'You certainly do,' said Joey, and screamed as I chased him inside, pretending to be mad.

✷ ♥ ♡

I went to bed meaning to get up shortly afterwards, but I was so tired that I fell asleep within seconds. Much later I woke with a jump. I looked at my phone. It was almost four o'clock. Poor Kate had been on her own in the field for ages.

I jumped up and threw on some clothes, then, just like the night before, I left a note for Mum and Dad, and tip-toed out of the house.

It was another clear night, and it was kind of peaceful walking along the quiet tree-lined road.

When I got to the tent I peeped through the flaps; Kate was asleep.

'Kate,' I whispered, trying not to frighten her.

She opened her eyes. 'You've been ages,' she said.

'Sorry,' I said. 'Now move over. I'm coming in.'

We lay there for a while without speaking. I looked out through the tent flaps and found the constellations that Kate had taught me about the night before.

Then Kate asked, 'What do you think will happen when Mr Phillips comes?'

'I don't know,' I said, not wanting her to know how worried I was about Mr Phillips.

'I bet he's an evil property developer,' said Kate. 'I bet he won't care about us, or about the tree, or about the protest. He'll find a way to get rid of us. Poor Jeremy is doomed.'

Something had been on my mind, and I felt like now might be the time to say it.

'Er ... Kate,' I began.

'What?'

'What if you told Mr Phillips about your dad?'

Kate sat up suddenly. 'What do you mean?' she asked so fiercely that it frightened me.

'Er, you know ... about how he used to bring you here when you were a little girl ... and how special this place was to the two of you ... and how he died ... you know ... all that stuff. Mr Phillips might ... you know ... feel sorry for you ... and he might decide not to cut down the tree.'

'No,' shouted Kate, her voice sounding really loud in the quiet of the night, 'I am *not* doing that.'

'But it might help Jeremy,' I said. 'It might be the only way to help Jeremy.'

'Can't you understand English? I said *no*.'

'But why?' I persisted.

She hesitated. 'Because ... because ...well because it just wouldn't be right. Dad wouldn't want me to use his memory like that. It would be disrespectful. Now I don't want to talk about it any more. OK?'

'OK,' I whispered.

I felt a bit cross with Kate. I was doing everything I could to save her special tree, and now she wouldn't help by doing the one thing that would surely sort it out once and for all.

But a few minutes later, I decided that wasn't fair. After all, what did I know?

I had a mum and a dad who loved me. (OK, so they'd kill me if they knew where I was right now, but basically, they loved me.)

I should probably be grateful.

I lay there looking at the stars, and after a while Kate whispered, 'Eva?'

'What?'

'Sorry for shouting at you.'

I smiled into the darkness. 'That's OK. If we didn't have the odd fight, we wouldn't be proper friends.'

Kate curled up like a puppy and sighed.

'Thanks, Eva,' she said, and then we went to sleep.

Chapter Twenty-Six

I woke up cold and hungry, but didn't like to
go away and leave Kate on her own.

I was really glad when I heard the sound of
Joey's out of tune whistling coming along the
lane.

'Breakfast is here,' he said, putting a basket on
to the blanket next to us. 'Your mum and dad
said they'll be along in a while, Eva, and I'll be
back too. I'm going to round up the troops.'

Kate grinned at him. 'Know what, Joey?' she
asked.

'What?'

'If I had a brother, I'd like one just like you.'

Joey went bright red, so I knew he was pleased.

Then he skipped off.

Soon afterwards Lily arrived. She was dressed a bit more suitably than the day before, but she still looked totally cool in jeans and a loose top. I was really glad that I was wearing Victoria's blue hoodie. Kate was still wearing her old tracksuit, which was by now dirty as well as raggy, but I was glad that she had used her fingers to flatten her hair a bit, and she'd put on Lily's hairband again.

Lily had a bag with her.

'Now, don't go taking offence,' she said to Kate, 'but I brought you some stuff – for a loan – like we said yesterday. And there's nothing pink or sparkly – I promise.'

Kate looked at her suspiciously, and said nothing as Lily pulled a pair of cropped denim trousers from the bag.

Lily held them towards Kate. 'Here,' she said. 'Try them on. I'd say you're about the same size as me.'

Kate took the trousers from Lily and stepped behind the tree. When she came back, we could see that the trousers fitted perfectly.

'Excellent,' said Lily.

Kate made a face.

'They're lovely, thanks, Lily, but they look a bit stupid with my old tracksuit top.'

Lily grinned.

'Not a problem,' she said, as she pulled a really nice casual top from the bag.

Seconds later Kate came from behind the tree again. The top and trousers looked great, but now that she was wearing short trousers, her old runners looked even worse than they had before.

Lily grinned again.

'I think I just might have thrown in a pair of flip-flops. Oh, yes, I did.'

She handed the cool, non-sparkly flip-flops to Kate, and watched as Kate took off her old runners, flung them to the ground, and slipped the flip-flops on to her feet. Her feet were kind of dirty, but no one mentioned that.

'Now stand up straight and let us look at you properly,' commanded Lily.

Kate did as she was told, and Lily and I gasped.

'You look totally different,' I said. 'You look beautiful.'

Kate went red.

'Thanks,' she said. 'And thanks, Lily.'

Lily smiled.

'You're welcome.'

Suddenly Kate's smile vanished.

'If you're lending me all this cool stuff, I should be lending you something back. That's the way it works, right?'

'Er ... sort of ... yes,' said Lily doubtfully, looking at Kate's discarded tracksuit, and the runners that were perched on the grass like they were getting ready to run away.

Kate picked up the two pieces of her tracksuit.

'Which one do you want, Lily? Top or bottom?

Or, since we're really good friends now, you can have both.'

Lily didn't answer. I put my head down. How stupid was Kate?

Suddenly Kate gave a big laugh.

'I'm kidding. Now that I think of it, I don't want to wear these any more, and I certainly don't expect you to.'

Lily gave an embarrassed smile.

'I knew that,' she said, and it didn't matter that we all knew she was lying.

Still Kate wasn't happy.

'I know you don't want my clothes, but I feel bad. I ought to give you something.'

Then she gave a sudden smile. She unzipped the pocket of her tracksuit bottoms, and pulled out a smooth white stone. She handed it to Lily.

'Here,' she said. 'You can have my favourite stone.'

I looked at Lily to see what she thought about this. She didn't seem to be the kind of girl who liked to borrow stones from her friends.

But Lily seemed entranced.

'It's perfect,' she said. 'And what are these lines?'

Kate leaned over and stroked the stone.

'It's a fossil. A creature died millions of years ago, and its skeleton left these marks on the stone.'

Lily gasped.

'That is so, so cool.'

Kate looked pleased.

'You can keep it if you like.'

Lily shook her head.

'No thanks. We're just lending remember.'

'OK,' said Kate. 'But I know a real good place to find these. Maybe the three of us can go there some time?'

Lily and I nodded happily.

Lily reached in to her bag again.

'Do you want me to paint your toe-nails for you Kate?'

Kate backed away.

'No way. Do that and I'll make you borrow my tracksuit.'

We all laughed and then we sat on the old faded rug and waited for the day to begin properly.

Chapter Twenty-Seven

By eleven o'clock the field was practically full – like there was some kind of carnival going on. All of the people from the day before were there, along with about fifty others. Some girls from Kate's school showed up, and they chatted with her for a while. I could see that Kate was embarrassed, but pleased too. There were loads of tourists, along with people I knew from the village. Hans was sitting on a blanket playing his guitar, accompanied by two American girls, one with a tin-whistle and the other with a banjo.

There was lots of laughing and chatting, and I began to wonder about all the different people, from different parts of the world who had come together to help us.

Then I heard a familiar voice from behind the hedge.

'Hey, Eva, come and give us a hand. Do you know how hard it is to wheel a wheelchair through a field?'

It couldn't be.

But it was.

Maggie was laughing, and Ruby's face matched her name, as she struggled to wheel her mother's chair across the rough grass.

I grabbed Kate's arm and raced over to the edge of the field.

I hugged Maggie and Ruby and then turned to Kate.

'This is my friend Ruby, and her mum, Maggie,' I said.

'You mean Madame Margarita?' said Kate laughing.

Maggie put her hands over her face. 'Do you

have to tell everyone, Eva?' she asked, but I knew that she was laughing too.

Between the three of us, we managed to manoeuvre Maggie's wheelchair into a nice spot, just near Jeremy's trunk.

Maggie opened the hold-all she was carrying on her knees.

'I made flags,' she said. 'There should be one for everyone.'

As she spoke, she pulled out heaps of small yellow flags, each of which had a tiny tree drawn on them.

'They are totally amazing,' said Lily, as she waved one in the air, and then backed away as people rushed at her, all trying to get a flag for themselves.

While Joey and his friends distributed the flags, Ruby came and sat with Kate, Lily and me.

'What on earth are you doing here?' I asked.

'Mum phoned your dad last night, asking

about spare parts for the stairlift he fitted, and he told her what's been going on. And because I had a few days off from swimming camp, Mum and I decided to come here to support you. We got the first bus this morning.'

'But….' I began.

Ruby smiled.

'After all you did for Mum and me last year, it was the least we could do.'

Everyone stared at me then, and I felt totally embarrassed – and a little bit pleased.

Kate nudged me as a man and a woman walked in to the field.

'I know them,' she said. 'They work on the local newspaper.'

The man and woman spoke to a few people who all pointed towards me.

They walked towards us, and the man introduced himself.

'I understand this is all your doing,' he said.

I nodded.

'Sort of. Well, it's me and Kate really.'

Kate pulled Lily over.

'And Lily too,' she said. 'She's our fashion consultant.'

The man took out his notebook, and asked us loads of questions about the tree, and why we were protesting. I didn't dare to mention Kate's dad, and wasn't surprised when she didn't either.

Then the woman asked if she could take a picture, and tried to get everyone to organize themselves into an orderly group. Kate, Lily and I were pushed to the front.

'Lucky I've got my best clothes on,' whispered Kate, making Lily and me giggle.

At last the group was arranged and we all had to stand still while the photographer took loads of pictures.

Just as the newspaper people left, Chainsaw Man arrived. He came straight over to Kate and me, avoiding Miley's wife who was standing leaning on a stick, looking menacing.

'This can still end peacefully,' he said. 'We can forget about what's happened if you all just walk away.'

'I can't walk,' said Maggie.

Chainsaw Man turned and saw her wheelchair for the first time. He went so red that I almost felt sorry for him.

'I can push you if you like,' he said in the end.

Maggie smiled. 'That's very kind of you, but I think I'll stay here for a while.'

Chainsaw Man then turned to me.

'Mr Phillips just phoned me,' he said. 'He's on his way. He'll be here any minute. This could be your last chance to give in gracefully.'

'Thanks,' I said. 'But, no thanks.'

Then I had a sudden thought. 'Whose side are you on anyway?' I asked.

Chainsaw Man shrugged.

'I'm not paid to take sides. I just do my job. But—'

'But what?' asked Kate.

'Mostly I cut down half-dead trees, or ones that are in danger of being blown down. But this is a strong, healthy tree, and part of me feels it's very wrong to damage it. I have to admire what you kids are doing in trying to save it.'

'So don't cut it down,' said Kate.

The man shrugged.

'If I refuse, Mr Phillips will just find someone else to do it. I lose the business, and the tree will still be gone.'

What he said made sense, but I still didn't like it.

Before I could think of something to say, a sleek black car drew up at the entrance to the field. It was closely followed by a police car. A man in an expensive-looking suit got out of the first car, and three policemen got out of the police car. There was no sign of Gerry, the local policeman. Everyone gasped when they saw that the policemen were dressed in full riot gear, like they were going to deal with hundreds of knife-wielding hooligans, instead of a group of peaceful people who were just trying to save a tree.

The man spoke to the policemen. They waited by their car, while he walked towards us.

The music stopped, and there was no chanting. There was no sound at all except for the squeak of the man's shiny shoes on the grass, and the singing of the birds from the highest branches of the tree.

The man stopped walking and gazed at us.

'Who's in charge here?' he asked in a calm, powerful voice.

I was glad that no one answered, but it didn't do me much good, as everyone betrayed me by staring in my direction. Mum and Dad moved from the centre of the crowd, and stood beside me. Mum took my hand and squeezed it tightly. Dad put his arm around my shoulder.

The man walked over and stopped in front of me. He was so close that I could see the tiny stitching on the collar of his suit. I could smell his expensive aftershave.

'Let me introduce myself,' he said. 'My name is Jason Phillips. Maybe you would be so kind as to explain what you are doing here in my field.'

I was so frightened, I couldn't think of anything to say. Dad squeezed my shoulder in encouragement, and even though that made me feel a small bit better, I still couldn't find the courage to open my mouth.

'I'll tell you if you like,' shouted Miley's wife, stepping forward and waving her stick like she wanted to kill someone with it.

Miley pulled her back.

'I knew I should have left you at home,' he muttered.

Suddenly Kate was whispering in my ear.

'This is our chance, Eva,' she said. 'You have to talk to Mr Phillips. You have to make him understand. You have to help me. You have to help Jeremy.'

And suddenly it was like Eva Gordon wasn't standing in that field any more. It was like someone braver and cleverer than me had stepped into my shoes, and was using my mouth to say words that I would never have thought of on my own.

'I'll tell you what's going on, Mr Phillips,' I said, as I pulled away from Mum and Dad, and stepped forward. 'We're trying to save this tree. This tree has been here for more than a hundred years. It was here before I was born – even before you were born. This tree means something to all of us – something that your holiday home never will. So basically we're not going anywhere. We're going to stay here for as long as it takes. And trust me, we're very patient people.'

Just then Miley's wife wriggled away from her husband.

'I'm not patient,' she said. 'Just say the word and I'll sort this man out once and for all.'

Mum patted her shoulder.

'Thanks very much,' she said, 'but I think we can leave this to Eva.'

Miley's wife let herself be led to the back of the crowd, and Mr Phillips spoke again.

'You were saying?'

My hands were shaking, and I realised that tears were streaming down my face. I heard a sound behind me, and saw that Mum and Dad were both wiping their eyes, and that Kate's eyes were sparkling strangely.

'It's very simple,' I said. 'You can threaten us all you like, but we are never, ever going to let you destroy this beautiful, precious, wonderful place.'

'Hear, hear,' shouted Miley's wife from the back of the crowd, and suddenly there was a chorus of cheers from everyone else. Joey and his friends jumped up and down and whistled, and everyone waved their flags madly.

At last the cheers died down, and Mr Phillips

stepped even closer to me. I knew he couldn't hurt me in front of all those people, but still I felt a cold stab of fear.

'What's your name, young lady?' he asked.

'Eva.' It came out like a squeak.

'Do you know what you are, Eva?' he asked.

I shook my head, afraid to speak.

'You're a credit to your parents, that's what.'

I wasn't sure I'd heard him properly, but still I didn't say anything. Mr Phillips continued. 'I have a girl just about your age, and do you know where she is now?'

This sounded like one of those questions that adults ask, that never seem to require answers, so I said nothing, and waited for him to continue.

'I'll tell you where she is. She's at home, sitting on her bed, straightening her hair, talking on the phone, and watching rubbish on TV.'

So basically she's just like me – the real me.

Mr Phillips kept talking.

'I'm ashamed to say that my daughter is

nothing at all like you. You are a wonderful, brave and principled girl to stand up for what you believe in. You're eloquent, you're strong, you're—'

Miley's wife stepped forward again.

'Enough about her already,' she cried. 'What about the tree?'

Mr Phillips actually smiled.

'Oh, the tree,' he said. 'I'd nearly forgotten about that, I was so busy praising this remarkable young lady.'

Dad stepped forwards and patted my shoulder, as Mr Phillips continued.

'Suddenly I'm ashamed that I ever considered destroying this wonderful tree – I don't know what I was thinking of. This is a very big field. I'll talk to the planning people and I'm fairly sure I'll be able to find another place to build my house. I'll build far away from here so that you can all visit the tree any time you like. How does that sound?'

Miley's wife dropped her stick and ran over and hugged Mr Phillips, wrapping her filthy arms tightly around his neck. Mr Phillips endured it bravely, and when he managed to free himself, he came over and shook my hand.

'Well done, young lady,' he said.

Mum and Dad came up and hugged me.

'That's our daughter,' they said proudly, and Mr Phillips told them again what a credit I was to them, while I just stood there grinning, hoping that they'd remember this moment the next time I was in trouble.

✭   ♥   ♡

An hour later, Mr Phillips and the policemen had left, and most of the rest of us were feasting on the mountain of food that Lily's mum had brought.

Once the food was gone, people sat around enjoying the sunshine.

Friedrich gave Joey and his friends the soccer

lesson he had promised them. I looked over just as Joey scored a goal. Friedrich gave him a high-five and Joey looked like he was going to explode with happiness.

I chatted to Ruby and Maggie, while Hans taught Kate and Lily how to play some chords on his guitar.

Mum was talking about chickens with anyone who would listen, and Dad was looking at endless photos on a Japanese man's very fancy phone.

Before long, it was time for Maggie and Ruby to catch the bus back home. I went to the edge of the field with them.

'Thanks so much for coming,' I said. 'It was really lovely to see you both.'

'It's our pleasure,' said Maggie. 'And know what, Eva? You'll go a long, long way.'

Ruby sighed.

'I thought you'd given up fortune-telling, Mum.'

Maggie slapped her daughter lightly on the arm.

'Don't be so cheeky,' she said. 'You don't need to be a fortune-teller to see that Eva has a bright future ahead of her.'

I leaned down and hugged her.

'Thanks, Maggie,' I whispered.

'Any time,' she said.

I went back over to the tree where Hans and Friedrich were handing out little cards with their names and addresses on them.

'Come visit us at any time,' said Hans.

'We will be showing you the wonders of Essen,' said Friedrich.

Miley's wife raced over. 'Give me one of them,' she said. 'I love travelling and I have lots of time on my hands. I could stay for ages and ages.'

Hans shoved the last of the cards into his back pocket. 'So sorry lady,' he said. 'Cards all used up. May I give you this lovely photograph of my dog?'

He shoved the picture into her hands and both men almost ran from the field.

The Japanese tourists solemnly bowed to everyone. Then they handed each person a tiny, folded paper bird.

'Is crane,' they said. 'For good luck.'

There were lots of hugs and kisses and laughter and even a few tears as people began to drift away. Soon only Kate, Lily and I were left.

We sat on the rug and looked at the trampled grass, and the last few flags, fluttering from Jeremy's branches.

'I have to go,' said Lily after a while. 'Mum's taking me in to town to buy me a new school uniform.'

The mention of school uniform brought me back to reality. I'd almost forgotten that the real world was going on without me, while I was hanging out in the country and saving trees with Kate.

Lily hugged us both and went off.

So it was just like before – Kate, Jeremy and me.

Chapter Twenty-Eight

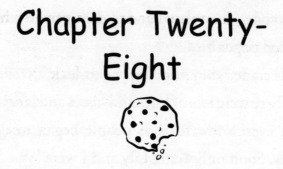

'What do you want to do?' I asked Kate. 'Jeremy is safe now, so it's OK to leave him for a while.'

Kate didn't reply.

'Want to go for a walk on the beach?' I asked.

Kate shook her head.

'Or to that place you showed me where the blackberries grow? Some of them might be ripe by now.'

Kate shook her head again.

'No. Let's just stay here.'

I thought I understood. The place had been so busy for the last few days, maybe she just wanted to relax and enjoy it now.

Maybe she wanted some quiet time to think about her dad.

The afternoon passed very slowly. It was sunny and warm, and for ages, Kate and I lay on the rug and watched the leaves fluttering over our heads in the gentle breeze.

I tried to talk to Kate but she was unusually quiet – quieter than I had ever seen her before.

'Isn't it great that we managed to save Jeremy?' I said for the tenth time, still excited by what we had managed to do. 'We took Mr Phillips on and we won! That is *so* totally amazing.'

'Yes,' said Kate, like it was no big deal, like we saved trees every day of our lives.

'You should be happy,' I said. 'Aren't you happy?'

'Yes, I'm happy,' said Kate in the saddest voice I'd ever heard.

Suddenly I couldn't take any more. I sat up.

'What's going on here, Kate?' I asked.

'Things have turned out exactly the way you wanted. We've just done something incredible. We've saved Jeremy from being chopped into firewood. We've changed the course of history. Kids who aren't even born yet will be able to sit here because of what we've done. And you're lying there with a long face, like it's the worst day of your life.'

Kate sat up but she didn't look at me.

'Eva, there's something I have to tell you,' she said.

'So tell me.'

Kate shook her head. 'I don't know if I can.'

I sighed. 'Just tell me already.'

She shook her head again. 'It's very hard. You see ... I'm not used to having a friend ... and ...'

'And talking to your friends isn't supposed to be hard,' I said impatiently.

'But it *is* hard, because when I tell you this, you won't want to be my friend any more. You're going to hate me.'

I had no idea what was going on, but I had a horrible, scared feeling in my stomach.

I forced a laugh. 'What could be that bad?'

Kate took a deep breath. 'I should have told you ages ago, but I didn't know how.'

I grabbed her arms, forcing her to look at me, but she quickly lowered her eyes.

'Tell me.'

'I told you a terrible lie, Eva,' she said. 'My dad wasn't killed by a truck.'

I was relieved. That wasn't such a bad lie. If my dad had died, maybe I'd want to exaggerate a bit about the details too.

'That's OK,' I said. 'Why don't you tell me how it really happened?'

Kate jumped to her feet, shaking herself free of my grip.

'That's the thing,' she said fiercely. 'My dad didn't die at all.'

At first I couldn't take it in properly.

'But he …,' I began, but I didn't know how to go on.

Kate continued. 'Dad's not dead. He just went away.'

'He what?'

'You heard me. He went away.'

Now it was my turn to be angry. I could hardly believe what she'd just said.

'You *lied* to me,' I shouted. 'Everything you told me was a lie. You just wanted me to feel sorry for you. You …'

I felt so stupid – how dare Kate trick me like that?

Kate interrupted. 'That's not the way I meant it. I—'

Now I interrupted her. 'I was kind to you. I helped you to save Jeremy. I—'

'And you only helped me because you thought my father had died? What kind of friend does that make you?'

Now there were tears in my eyes. From the

sound of her voice, I thought Kate might have been crying too, but I didn't want to look at her. I didn't want to see her.

'At least I'm not the kind of friend who makes up stupid lies about dead fathers,' I said quietly, and I began to walk away.

Kate didn't try to follow me.

✫   ♥   ♡

By the time I got home, I could hardly see, I was crying so much.

'Here comes our little heroine,' said Mum, as I pushed open the kitchen door. I just had time to notice the big banner, saying WELL DONE EVA, made out of pages torn from Joey's sketch pad.

Then Mum saw my face, and rushed over to me.

'Eva, what on earth has happened?' she cried. 'Did that man change his mind? Is he going to cut down the tree after all?'

'No,' I shouted. 'He's not going to cut down the tree, even though I wish he would. I wish he'd chop and chop until there was nothing left except leaves and sawdust.'

'I don't understand, Eva,' said Mum. 'What's going on? Is it Kate? Has something happened to Kate?'

I shook my head, 'No, unfortunately nothing has happened to Kate. She's alive and well – just like her father.'

Dad and Joey came in then. When Dad saw how upset I was, he came and put his arm around me. Joey patted my back, like I was a baby.

'What's happened, love?' asked Dad.

Mum answered for me.

'She's had some kind of falling out with her friend.'

'Kate is *not* my friend,' I shouted. 'I am never, ever going to talk to her again.'

'I know you don't really mean that,' said

Mum. 'But what were you saying about Kate's father?'

I wiped my eyes.

'It was all lies. Kate made the whole thing up. There was no injured bird, no truck, no accident – the whole thing was one big made-up story. Her father just went away – and I don't blame him, since he had such a horrible daughter.'

'Eva!' said Mum, but I ignored her.

'Kate told us all a big load of lies, just so we'd feel sorry for her,' I said. 'And the worst thing is, I believed her! I believed every single stupid, lying word.'

'We all believed her,' said Dad.

'Yes, but you weren't her friend. I was supposed to be her friend. How could she lie to her friend?'

And then at the thought of it, I started to cry again.

'I'm going up to my room,' I said. 'And I don't want to be disturbed.'

Mum and Dad looked at each other, but they stood back and watched as I went upstairs.

I threw myself on to my bed and cried until my head hurt, and my throat felt like someone was sticking sharp needles all over it.

And then I fell asleep.

✩   ♥   ♡

I woke up to see Mum standing at the end of my bed.

'I've brought you up your tea,' she said.

'I'm not hungry.'

Mum put the plate on the locker, and sat down on my bed.

'I know you're upset, Eva,' she said.

'Upset isn't a big enough word for the way I feel,' I said.

Mum stroked my hair.

'Kate might have her reasons. It can't be nice for her, being abandoned by her dad, and by her mum. She—'

'It's not nice for *me* being lied to. I really thought she was my friend. I thought I could trust her. And all the time she was lying.'

Mum sighed. 'Why don't you give her a chance? You could go over there and talk to her. I'll go with you if you like.'

'I am *never* going over there. I am *never* going to have anything to do with her again. I wish she was dead. Just like her father. Or just like her father isn't,' I corrected myself..

Mum sighed.

'You don't mean that, Eva,' she said.

'I do. I wish I'd never met Kate. I wish I was at home with Victoria and Ruby and Ella, my *real* friends. I wish this whole stupid summer had never happened.'

Mum leaned over and hugged me. 'You poor thing,' she said. 'Why don't you come on downstairs? I've made a lemon cake – your favourite.'

'Thanks, Mum,' I said. 'But I think I'll just

stay here for a while.'

Mum stood up.

'OK,' she said. 'But if you want to talk some more just give me a call.'

When she was gone, I sat up and ate the food she had left for me. Then I lay down and closed my eyes and cried some more.

Chapter Twenty-Nine

When I woke up the next morning, I had a headache. I had hardly slept all night, and when I did, my sleep was haunted by horrible, dark, ugly dreams. I kept dreaming that Kate was laughing at me for believing her lies.

I dragged myself downstairs where Mum, Dad and Joey were having breakfast.

Dad was reading the local paper.

'Look. We're famous. We're on the front page,' he said.

I took the paper from him. It was the group photo from the day before. There we all were, grinning happily. Kate's arm was around my shoulder, and mine was around hers – like we were very best friends.

I handed the paper back without a word.

'Aren't you happy any more about saving the tree?' asked Joey. 'Do you need me and the lads to help you to save something else?'

'Shhh, Joey,' said Mum. 'It's complicated. Eva's a bit upset, that's all. Now eat up your breakfast.'

Just as I was pouring myself a bowl of cereal, there was a loud knock at the door. I got such a fright, I held the cereal packet over the overflowing bowl until Joey said, 'Wow, you must really be hungry.'

As I tried to shovel the cereal back into the packet with my hands, there was another knock.

'Who could that be?' said Dad.

'Maybe it's a TV station wanting to interview Eva about the tree,' said Joey getting up.

'If it's Kate, I'm not here,' I said quickly.

'But you are here,' said Joey. 'Am I supposed

to tell her a lie?'

'I don't care,' I replied. 'You can tell her anything you like. You can tell her I've been run over by a truck – not that anyone except me would believe such a stupid lie.'

'Eva!' said Mum in a shocked voice.

'OK, OK,' I said. 'Don't tell her I've been run over by a truck. Tell her I've gone off to make some new friends. Some *real* friends.'

Seconds later Joey was back.

'It's Martha,' he said. 'So I didn't have to tell any lies. And she wants to talk to you, Eva.'

I felt like running upstairs and hiding under my bed, but one look at Mum and Dad told me that wasn't really an option.

Martha was leaning against the garden wall.

'What do you want?' I said, but not too rudely.

'Kate was afraid to come over herself, but she really wants to talk to you,' she said.

'Well, I don't want to talk to her.'

Martha sighed, suddenly looking very old and very tired.

'Kate told me what happened between you two. She told you a very stupid lie, and I can see why you're upset, but ... well ... can you try to understand her? She's had a hard time. She never knew her mum properly, and she hasn't really got over her dad's leaving. I've done my best, but I know I've never been a very good replacement. And Kate has been so happy this summer, since she met you. It's the first time since her father left that she's seemed like a normal, carefree young girl. And ... can't you make an old lady happy by talking to her?'

And what could I say to that?

'All right,' I said slowly. 'I'll talk to her. But that's all. OK?'

Martha gave me a watery smile.

'Thank you. You're a good lass,' she said.

I followed Martha as she walked very slowly down the small road that led from our house to hers. As we came close to her house, Kate suddenly stepped out from a bush, making me jump.

'I'll leave you two to it,' said Martha, walking slowly into her house.

I looked at Kate. She was back in one of her old tracksuits, and her hair was all messy. She looked just like she had the first day we met, all scruffy and defensive and silent.

'So you want to talk?' I said.

She nodded.

'Yes, but not here. Let's walk up to the field – to the Island of Dreams.'

I felt like hitting her. I'd thought of that field as such a special place, but now it was all spoiled because of Kate's lies.

But still I followed her.

I walked a few steps behind Kate as she led the familiar way. The field was empty, and only the flattened grass showed that anything unusual had happened there recently.

Kate went and sat against Jeremy, and because I felt stupid standing up, I sat down too, facing her.

'So start talking,' I said, keen to get it over with so I could escape from Kate forever.

When Kate started to speak, her voice was so low that I had to lean in close so I could hear her.

'My mum did go away when I was a baby,' she said.

'So you did manage to tell me something that was true,' I said in a hard voice. 'What a surprise.'

Kate gave me a hurt look, but I ignored it. After all, who was the injured party here?

Then she continued. 'And of course, I often missed having a mum, but I had a dad, so things didn't seem too bad. But Dad didn't have a job, and we hadn't much money, so we had to live with Martha. And sometimes things were fine, and we had lovely times together. All the stuff

I told you about camping and having picnics near Jeremy, that was all true.'

I made a face, which Kate ignored, and then she went on, 'But sometimes Dad and Martha used to have terrible fights. There was loads of shouting and banging of stuff, and slamming doors.'

That sounded a bit like my house on a good day, but I didn't feel like sharing that with Kate.

'And then one day, when I was ten, there was this really, really bad row, and Dad went in to his room and started to pack up all his stuff. He'd done that a few times before, so I wasn't too worried at first. I thought he'd just calm down, and later on we'd all laugh about it. But then he kept on packing, until everything he owned was crammed into two big suitcases. He sat me down and told me that he was leaving. I was crying, but he told me that he had to get away, or else he'd go crazy. He said he was going to England, and that he'd get a job, and find a nice place for us both to live. He said he'd find a lovely house with a big garden, with swings and a climbing frame. I said I didn't want swings and a climbing frame. I said I didn't care where we lived. I just wanted to go with him. But he wouldn't let me. That evening he left. And he never came back.'

I thought she was finished, but while I was wondering what to say, she continued. 'And will I tell you the worst thing?'

I didn't answer, so she said, 'When I was small, I used to ask why Mum left, and Dad said that it was because she didn't have time to get to know me. He said that if she'd known what a great kid I was, Mum would never, ever have left me. And then he left. That meant … that meant … he mustn't have thought I was a great kid any more.'

By now, huge, fat tears were rolling down Kate's face, and I knew for sure that she was telling the truth this time.

I forgot how angry I had been with Kate for lying to me. All I could think of was the poor girl crying, and begging her father not to leave her.

'And ... and ... does he ever write, or call ... or ...?' I asked.

'He never calls – maybe because he's afraid to talk to Martha. He does write sometimes. He sends me a card on my birthday.'

'Well, that's good, isn't it?'

Kate gave a small unhappy laugh. 'Is it? Would you be happy if all you ever got from your dad was a card, with a London postmark and no return address?'

I put my head down.

How could I guess what it was like to be Kate?

How could I imagine my mum and dad just walking off and leaving me forever?

Suddenly I had an idea.

'You could trace him – and your mum. There are people who specialise in that kind of thing.

I've seen a programme on TV about it.'

Kate shook her head slowly.

'Mum and Dad know where I am. They just don't want to be with me. And for all I know, they could be back together. They could be living happily ever after with a new baby – one they both really love.'

Suddenly I remembered something else.

'So that's why Martha feels guilty. Your dad left because of a row with her. And now she takes it out on you.'

Kate shook her head.

'Not really. Martha does her best. She's only cranky some of the time'

I made a face.

'Like the day I went to get the tent from her.'

'Yeah, sorry about that.'

There was one more thing I had to know.

'Why didn't you tell me the truth? Why did you make up all that crazy stuff about the truck?'

It took Kate so long to answer that I had to

check to see that she hadn't fallen asleep. Then, after ages, she spoke.

'I never talk about my mum and dad, and when you don't have any friends, that's not really hard to do. But then you came along, and you were so nice to me, and at first, when you mentioned family, I just avoided the issue, and I thought I could get away with it. But then I went to your house for lunch that day and I saw you with your mum and dad, and you looked so happy together – like a perfect family from an ad or a soppy TV programme or something. And you were all so nice to Joey, and to me.'

'But Mum and I fight all the time,' I said. 'And Dad drives me crazy sometimes, and in the beginning, I couldn't stand to be in the same room as Joey.'

Kate gave a sad smile.

'It still looked perfect to me. And then when Joey asked about my family … I hadn't really planned to tell lies … I'd never told lies like that before. The words just sort of came out on their own. I couldn't stop them, and then I couldn't change them. I didn't know how to tell you that it was all made up, so I just kept on pretending – even though I was afraid all the time that Martha, or Lily or someone else would tell you what really happened.'

I still didn't understand.

'But why tell the lies in the first place?'

Now Kate spoke quickly.

'Because I couldn't bear to tell the truth. I was ashamed. I couldn't find the words to tell you that my mum and my dad both just walked away. That they didn't love me. That I wasn't worth loving.'

Poor Kate.

No wonder she didn't care how she looked, or what other people thought of her. She thought she was a waste of space, because her mum and dad had left.

Now tears came to my eyes. I scrunched over

and hugged Kate so tightly that I must have hurt her.

'It wasn't your fault,' I said fiercely. 'None of it was your fault. I don't know much about these things, and I've never met your parents, but your mum and dad must have had some kind of problem – something that made them leave. But it wasn't you – I know it wasn't you.'

Kate didn't answer. I could just hear her sobs, and I could feel the shoulder of my best t-shirt becoming damp from her tears.

A bit later, we both wiped our eyes, and lay back on the grass. Soon Kate was snoring softly, and not long afterwards, I fell asleep too.

It had been a very long few days.

Chapter Thirty

I woke up as a shadow crossed my face.

'That's not fair. If there's a sleepover party going on, why am I not invited?'

It was Lily. Kate and I sat up. Kate gave me a panicked look, and I tried to show her with a small shake of my head, that I hadn't told Lily the story of Kate's dad and the non-existent truck.

Her secrets and lies were all safe with me.

'So do you two have crazy plans for the day, or can we just do normal stuff like talking about clothes and lipstick?' asked Lily.

'If you leave out the lipstick,' said Kate. 'It's a deal.'

And the three of us laughed.

✦ ♥ ♡

The next few days were fun.

Kate took us to the place where she found her fossil, and we spent a whole afternoon searching for treasures.

Sometimes we went to the beach and hung out, and sometimes we sat in the Island of Dreams and leaned against Jeremy and talked about nothing.

Some days Kate wore the clothes that Lily had lent her, but when they were being washed, she was back to her old tracksuits. Lily offered her more stuff, and I offered to lend her some of my clothes, but Kate was too proud to take anything else – and I think she knew we didn't want any of her tracksuits in return!

'You need some more clothes,' said Lily one afternoon. 'Have you got any money Kate?'

Kate shook her head.

Lily sighed.

'Me neither. What about you Eva?'

I searched my pockets.

'I've got thirty-two cent,' I said.

'I wouldn't take your money anyway,' said Kate defiantly, showing traces of the girl she'd been at the start of the summer.

'Leave it to me,' said Lily. 'I'll think of something.'

One day we collected two huge buckets of blackberries, and carried them back to my house.

'You should make jam,' said Mum.

Lily's eyes sparkled.

'That's it,' she said. 'I have a plan.'

A few days later, we set up our stall on the busy road leading to the beach. We had pots and pots of blackberry jam, bunches of flowers picked from Kate's garden, and plates of chocolate buns that Martha had helped us to make.

'Leave the sales talk to me, girls,' I said when

everything was ready. 'I have lots of experience from helping Ruby on her vegetable stall.'

Lily giggled.

'Running market stalls, saving trees, is there anything you can't do, Eva?'

I shrugged.

'Probably not.'

'You can't tell the future,' said Kate, 'or you'd have known *this* was going to happen.'

As she spoke, she grabbed one of the flower jugs and emptied the water over my head.

I screamed and splashed her back. The three of us had a big water fight, until we were interrupted by the arrival of our first customer.

It was Chainsaw Man.

'Well, you're great enterprising girls, altogether,' he said, politely not mentioning the fact that the three of us were all giggling madly and had water dripping from our clothes and hair. Then he bought two pots of jam and a whole plate of chocolate buns.

By that afternoon, we were doing really well, and after three days we had earned what seemed like a fortune. Kate wanted to split it three ways, but Lily and I wouldn't let her.

'You got the flowers, you knew where to get the blackberries, and the chocolate buns came from your top-secret family recipe,' said Lily. 'So we're not taking any money.'

Kate put on her defiant face, but she didn't argue.

Lily's mum told us about a great clothes shop in the next town, where there was a really good sale on, so one morning the three of us set off on the bus. Lily and I helped Kate to pick out loads of clothes that really suited her – all cool and casual and non-sparkly.

Kate insisted on buying us each a present – a t-shirt for me, and a sweet little teddy-bear for Lily.

On the bus home, Lily sighed happily.

'Shopping is my all-time favourite thing,' she

said. 'When we get back to school, the other kids will think there's a new girl in our class, Kate.'

Kate grinned.

'There will be a new girl. I am a new girl.'

And in some ways, I felt like she was telling the truth.

✦ ❤ ♡

The weeks passed quickly. One day, Dad got a call to do some work at home for a few days. Before he left, Mum took me aside.

'You've shown amazing maturity lately, Eva,' she said. 'So if you want to go back with Dad and spend a few days at home, that would be fine with us.'

I hesitated. Victoria and Ella were both on holidays, and Ruby was away at swimming camp, but it wasn't just that.

'No,' I said in the end. 'Thanks, anyway, but I think I'll just stay here. Kate, Lily and I have stuff to do.'

Cathy never came back to the village after her trip to France, and Lily, Kate and I hung out together every day. Sometimes Kate had a distant, sad air about her, but mostly she was fine. I knew I couldn't make everything all right for her. I couldn't make her mum or dad come back, but in some small way, I felt like I had helped her.

☆ ♥ ♡

And so the summer slipped towards an end. The days got chillier, the evenings got darker, and gradually the tourists began to pack up their bags, ready to go back to their real lives.

Then came the day when we had to leave – the day I had once dreamed of, but which had now come too soon. I felt sad as I helped to pack and tidy up the house.

In the morning, Lily called over to say goodbye.

'Will you be here next summer?' she asked.

I looked at Mum and Dad.

'Please, please, please can we come here next year?' I begged.

They laughed.

Dad scratched his head and pretended to think.

'Oh yes,' he said. 'Holiday from hell? Isn't that what you said the first day?'

I made a face. 'Things are different now,' I said. 'Everything is different.'

'We can talk to Monica,' said Mum. 'And I think we could probably arrange something, for a week or two at least.'

'Please can I come with you?' asked Joey. 'Holidays with you are so much fun.'

I looked at his cute freckly face, and realised that sounded like a great idea.

'Please, Mum?' I said.

Mum laughed.

'If it's OK with your parents, Joey, then it

would be fine with us.'

'Yay,' said Joey as he skipped around the room, making us all laugh.

A few minutes later, Lily left, promising to keep in touch, and I went back to helping Mum and Dad.

Soon everything was done.

'I'm going to have a last cup of tea,' said Mum. 'So if you have anything left to do, Eva, now is the time to do it.'

I knew what she meant.

✧　♥　♡

I walked over to Kate's place. Martha met me at the door with a big bag of chocolate cookies.

'Just to say thank you,' she said.

Kate came out. She was wearing some of her new clothes and she looked really nice. Her hair had grown a bit longer, and she was wearing it the way Lily had shown her. I was wearing the t-shirt she had bought for me.

Suddenly we were both shy.

'I haven't got much time,' I said. 'But I want to go and say goodbye to Jeremy before I leave.'

I stopped and slapped my forehead.

'I can't believe I'm saying goodbye to a tree.'

Kate laughed.

'And you're calling a tree "Jeremy". You've been in the country too long, Eva – I think it's definitely time for you to go home.'

After that everything was OK. We walked to the field, and we both climbed the tree, sitting on the highest branches, like we did the first day Kate had taken me there.

We didn't say much. We just sat there, swaying in the breeze and watching the sunshine dancing on the water.

After a while, I heard Joey calling, 'Eva, time to go.'

Kate and I scrambled down from the tree.

'Walk back with me?' I said.

Kate shook her head quickly – but not quickly

enough. I could see tears glistening in her eyes.

'No thanks, Eva. I think I'll stay here for a bit.'

I tried to smile.

'It's not so bad. Maybe you could come and stay with me for a weekend. And Mum says we can come back here on holidays next year. And I'll call you sometimes, I promise.'

Kate brightened for a second.

'We've got computers at school. I can e-mail you if you like.'

I told her my e-mail address, and then there didn't seem to be anything else to say.

We hugged quickly, and I ran down the field, too sad to look back.

✦　♥　♡

Everything seemed different when I got back to the city, back to my real home. The tree in the front garden was just a tree, and I couldn't imagine ever giving it a name, or caring for it.

When we got inside, the house smelled different. With all the curtains closed, it was dark and gloomy. There was no air, almost like the house had been holding its breath, waiting for us to come back.

I carried my bag upstairs, and sat on my bed. Nothing seemed right any more. Nothing seemed real.

Just then the doorbell rang, and seconds later, loud footsteps on the stairs announced Victoria's arrival. I smiled. Victoria's phone was still broken, so we hadn't been in touch since the day she'd visited me on holidays. She didn't know anything about Kate or Lily, or about the campaign to save Jeremy.

Victoria burst into the room and practically knocked me down as she ran to hug me.

'Omigod, Eva, I'm so glad you're back. I've really missed you. And you must be glad to be back too. You must have been totally bored in the country. I bet not one single thing happened there. A few funny things happened here. One day, Ella and I—'

I laughed and held up my hand to stop her.

'You can tell me in a minute,' I said. 'But first make yourself comfortable. There's something I want to tell *you*.'

So Victoria sat on my bed, folded her arms, and listened carefully while I told her all about my friend Kate.

From spoilt princess
to pretty cool girl!

Rich, spoilt, high-maintenance Eva Gordon likes luxurious,
sophisticated things so when her parents cancel a holiday and get
rid of their expensive car, she can't understand why.

But when Eva's dad loses his job and she has to move house and
change schools, she realises things have changed forever. She's
determined to hate her new life. Then a chance visit to a fortune
teller gives her the idea that doing good may help her to turn things
back the way they were. Eva (with the help of best friend Victoria)
starts to help everyone she can — whether they want it or not! And
maybe being nice is helping Eva herself just as much …

Best friends NEED to be together. Don't they?

Poor Megan! Not only is she stuck with totally uncool parents, and a little sister who is too cute for words, but now her best friend, Alice, has moved away. Now Megan has to go to school and face the dreaded Melissa all on her own. The two friends hatch a risky plot to get back together. But can their secret plan work?

It's mid-term break and Megan's off to visit Alice.

Megan is hoping for a nice trouble-free few days with her best friend. No such luck! She soon discovers that Alice is once again plotting and scheming.
It seems that Alice's mum Veronica has a new boyfriend. The plan is to discover who he is, and to get rid of him!

Alice and Megan are together again!

They are both looking forward to their Confirmation, especially as their two families are going out to dinner together to celebrate.
But not even a meal can be simple when Alice is around as she decides to hatch a plan to get her parents back together ...

Best friends forever?

Megan can't wait to go away to Summer Camp with Alice!
It will be fantastic — no organic porridge, no school,
nothing but fun! But when Alice makes friends with
Hazel, Megan begins to feel left out.
Hazel's pretty, sophisticated and popular, and
Alice seems to think she's amazing.
Is Megan going to lose her very best friend?

Sunshine & yummy French food — sounds like the perfect holiday!

Megan's really looking forward to the summer holidays — her whole family is going to France, and best of all Alice is coming too! But when Alice tries to make friends with a local French boy things begin to get very interesting ...

Alice and Megan are starting secondary school.

New subjects, new teachers and new friends — it's going to take a bit of getting used to.

And when Megan meets Marcus, the class bad-boy who's always in trouble, but doesn't seem to care, things really start to get complicated.

At least she has Home Ec class with Alice — the worst cook in the school — to look forward to, so school's not all bad!

How much should you give up for your best friend?

Alice has a good chance of winning the school essay competition — and the prize is four months in France!

Megan loves writing essays, but she'd hate to go away for four months alone! She doesn't want Alice to go either — why would anyone want to go abroad without her best friend? But Alice seems determined to win ...

Get cooking with Alice & Megan!

Alice and Megan are writing a cookbook. But Alice is not
the world's the greatest cook, so could it be a recipe for
disaster? Well, not with Megan's help ....
This fun-filled cookbook is packed with brilliant recipes.
Why not wake up to French toast and tropical smoothies?
Or go to school with raspberry muffins and pasta salad?
Or snack on s'mores and quesadillas? Or impress your
friends with home-made burgers followed by ice cream
with toffee sauce? All this and more included!

Brilliant Breakfasts . Lucky Lunchboxes . Super Snacks . Marvel-
lous Main Courses . Delicious Desserts . Cakes & Cookies.